Lyla's Encore

Mary Jackson Meyer

TRILOGY CHRISTIAN PUBLISHERS
TUSTIN, CA

Trilogy Christian Publishers
A Wholly Owned Subsidiary of Trinity Broadcasting Network
2442 Michelle Drive
Tustin, CA 92780

For information, address Trilogy Christian Publishing

Rights Department, 2442 Michelle Drive, Tustin, Ca 92780.

For information about special discounts for bulk purchases, please contact Trilogy Christian Publishing.

Manufactured in the United States of America

10 9 8 7 6 5 4 3 2 1

Library of Congress Cataloging-in-Publication Data is available.

ISBN 978-1-64773-530-2

ISBN 978-1-64773-531-9 (ebook)

Contents

Chapter 1. 1
Chapter 2. 17
Chapter 3. 27
Chapter 4. 41
Chapter 5. 51
Chapter 6. 59
Chapter 7. 63
Chapter 8. 73
Chapter 9. 79
Chapter 10. 95
Chapter 11. 109
Chapter 12. 121
Chapter 13 133
Chapter 14. 143
Chapter 15 149
Chapter 16. 163
Chapter 17 173
Chapter 18. 181
Chapter 19. 197
Chapter 20 207

Chapter 21. 215
Chapter 22. 225
Chapter 23. 235
Chapter 24. 243
Chapter 25. 253
Chapter 26. 269
Chapter 27. 285
Chapter 28. 297
Epilogue. 307

Thank you, Phil Jackson, for introducing me to the hilarity of retirement living.

Thank you, William Meyer, for giving me the opportunity to live it out!

Chapter 1

Betts Knight, short for Beatrice Knight, smeared SPF 30 sunscreen across her shoulders and around the straps of her tankini before sliding into an orthopedic chaise lounge. She was poolside at the Arcadia Retirement Village, in south-central Florida where all deck chairs were Aruba-blue and equipped with built-in lumbar support, padded headrests, and accompanied by a little black button on the arm rest that raised or lowered her feet. The pool was just one of many amenities in the over fifty-five community. Betts leaned back and closed her eyes behind her tortoise shell sunglasses hoping to drift into an afternoon nap but the steady whir of golf carts rolling by carrying self-appointed landscaping specialists altered her plan. Unrestrained retirees felt compelled to shout advice to landscapers laying a new sprinkler system in the gardens between the shuffleboard court and pool deck. Betts pulled her sunglasses down the bridge of her nose and looked out over the top at the commotion. It was becoming obvious that her nap would have to wait until she returned home in a day or two.

She didn't meet the age requirement to be a resident in the gated community, but Momma did. Betts had driven into town earlier that week to help Momma settle into her new surroundings. She took note of the Piggly Wiggly as she drove south on Highway 70. Her mother was not especially handy in the kitchen, but Betts would be sure to stock her cupboards with required essentials including coffee and flavored creamer. She made a mental note to show her mother how to turn on the coffee maker.

The rural town of Arcadia was a far cry from the life to which Momma was accustomed. Betts had driven past cattle ranches and orange groves before seeing the "Welcome to Arcadia" sign on Rural Highway 70. The town, proper, was graced with four stop lights on the main drag one of which was strategically positioned on the corner of Highway 70 and the entrance to "The Village" where Momma would be staying. Betts had slowed to a stop when the light turned yellow, she flipped the blinker and as she waited, counted seven golf carts, bound for the Walmart parking lot scooting across the road in front of her.

The travelers seemed to Betts to be escapees from the retirement village, all filing by in a neat row, one behind the other and dressed in what may have been the acceptable attire for village residents. Men and women were all donned in brightly colored Florida t-shirts, sun visors and support stockings with sensible shoes. A wave of worry flooded her. Perhaps moving her mother here was a mistake. Momma did not accede to acceptable. She would rather die than be caught alive in sensible shoes and logoed T-shirts. Nor did she drive a golf cart, Momma drove a Porsche.

However, early childhood memories of counting train cars from the back seat brought a smile to Betts's face as she waited for red to turn to green. Despite what might become her mother's exceptions with the local customs, Betts knew the Village was just what Momma needed for a full recovery. She checked the dashboard clock; it seemed a particularly long light. The red waited patiently to change until the full train of golf carts was safely on the far side of the four lanes. But it was this pause that provided Betts a moment of deep breathing strengthening her resolve to keep her mother concealed, here, in the Arcadia Retirement Village.

A four-foot high stucco wall marked the divide between Village property and Highway 70. A replica of the Venus De Milo stood on a pedestal in the middle of the boulevard that divided the entrance lane from the exit. Someone had draped a winter scarf around her shoulders and pulled a stocking cap over her ears reminding all that Arcadia Retirement Village was a winter haven for snowbirds dodging the frigid temperatures up north. It was an odd sight, like a college prank during finals week, but Betts's attention was quickly drawn to a giant seashell sign next to Venus and she smiled as she read,

"Welcome to
Arcadia Retirement Village
Active retirement living for seniors on the go!"

Betts counted four more golf carts in her rearview mirror lining up at the traffic light as she crept about fifty yards up the entrance lane to the Village gate. She eased her SUV over a speed bump that forced the 15 mile-per-hour speed limit.

The stucco wall that bordered the front of the Village continued up the drive to the gate that was raised only for code carrying residents and their welcomed guests. On first consideration, Betts thought maybe the four feet of stucco surrounding the community was there for safety's sake, a barrier to keep all who weren't residents "out." However, surveying the parade of golf carts scooting into the grass and dodging the apparently ill-placed speed bump to ramp up over 15 mph, she began to think it might be just the opposite; more than likely, it was there to keep the residents "in." She doubted that any of the fifty-five plus crowd motoring about would be nimble enough to scale the four feet of stucco and, of course, as far as her mother was concerned, that was for the best. She breathed a silent prayer that somehow, the stucco barrier would keep Lyla Fontaine, now Anne Knight, out of trouble.

She punched in her mother's code at the gate and it lifted obediently, giving her clearance to pull forward and follow the GPS directions through the winding lanes lined with budding magnolia trees and cottages painted an array of Florida colors including ocean blue, flamingo pink, and sunrise yellow. The homes were small but lovely, trimmed in white looking crisp and clean. Betts turned onto Sunset Lane where each cottage flaunted a front porch with room enough for two chairs and a small table making the whole scene serene and inviting.

Betts had been summoned to the Village by Momma. Being the only child, it was her duty to answer the call and come to her mother's aid. Not that Lyla Fontaine couldn't afford to hire help, in fact, she had the means to purchase her own hospital wing fully armed with staff and equipment if she wanted, but Lyla always found great comfort in motivating her one and only by artfully mapping out a guilt trip Betts couldn't maneuver out of. So, when Momma called, Betts came, immediately.

Lyla Fontaine, who now was to be introduced by her middle name, Anne, and her surname, Knight, had been a Bond girl in the 60's. Bond, as in *James Bond*. As an attractive buxom teenager, wearing the buxom part of herself quite proudly, Lyla was discovered by a talent agent in Swartz Creek, Michigan while waitressing at a soda fountain. Hence the last name *Fontaine*. Back in the days when one could be trusted when introducing themselves as an agent representing Tenor and Young Talent Agency, Lyla jumped at the opportunity and signed on the dotted line almost immediately. Like most high school graduates, young Loise Anne Knight had dreamed of leaving her small-town drudgery to head for the glamor of Hollywood she had seen in the magazines.

Anne, taking on the persona of Lyla, was a natural in front of the camera. Small roles grew to supporting roles until the Bond enterprise offered her a contract and she became a big screen favorite.

The camera loved Lyla Fontaine almost as much as the crowds. She was beautiful as well as buxom, spunky, and sassy, yet remained genteel even as the limelight grew brighter. Lyla's trademark became her charming smile that revealed a small but noticeable space between her two front teeth. With long blond curls that splashed around her shoulders, she was the embodiment of the "girl next door." Everywhere she went the crowds begged her to flash that smile in their direction as cameras clicked and flashbulbs blazed.

Lyla's career boasted quite the list of handsome leading men whose arms she would grace for a red-carpet stroll on her way to receiving an Oscar, but she refused to get involved in a serious relationship. She was in demand as an actress, one movie after another. Her box office hits not only rendered her the choicest of roles but even led her to Grauman's Chinese Theater and the Walk of Fame on Hollywood Boulevard where her handprints were forever cemented into history.

During her extensive and successful career, she took only one short sabbatical from acting: the year of 1976. Everything was cancelled from her schedule as Lyla hid from sight and claimed a year of renewal. The press wrote stories speculating about her much-needed time away filled with privacy and fresh air to clear her head and renew her creative energies. No interviews were granted.

When she quietly reappeared unannounced to her fans at the Los Angeles Christmas tree lighting, Lyla Fontaine was pushing a baby stroller carrying her three-month-old daughter. The child was introduced as Beatrice, named after Lyla's dedicated assistant and friend, Beatrice Brown. The adorable child, Beatrice, who by kindergarten was nicknamed Betts, was given her mother's family surname, Knight. Though Lyla introduced the infant Betts to her birth father, and he graced her with a generous trust fund, his name never appeared in writing, even on her birth certificate, and his identity was never made public.

Although Lyla bore the pain of giving her heart secretly to one of the handsome leading men resulting in motherhood, she wore her new title gracefully and resolutely. Lyla faced the scrutiny determined to hold her head up and move forward with her daughter in tow. While her career remained her focus and first love, Betts became her movie star momma's second: second focus, second love. That was life for Lyla Fontaine and Betts Knight. It wasn't the fairytale one reads about, but as a child, it was all Betts knew and as a celebrity mother, it was all Lyla could give. Despite it all, Betts loved her mother, the great Lyla Fontaine, even more than Lyla's fans.

In the 70's it was quite chic for the rich and famous to hire nannies trained by NANA, the *North American Nanny Association*. Staying ever in the limelight, stylish and sophisticated, Lyla took the advice of her colleagues and friends and hired a gifted nanny for Betts. Maybelle Studer, a wonderfully southern, African American woman, NANA trained, moved into the east suite of the Fontaine mansion where Betts would spend most of her childhood years growing up.

Maybelle Studer came highly recommended and Lyla Fontaine would settle for nothing less for her second love. Maybelle, the elder of the two women by nearly ten years, didn't compare in physical beauty to Lyla, and Lyla didn't compare to the physical stature of Maybelle. Betts could remember her momma leaving the house and disappearing beyond the size of her nanny as she walked out the door. In fact, at just the right angle, Betts could even lose sight of the Porsche that her momma climbed into. But Maybelle was larger in emotion as well, she was soft and kind and loved Betts as her first love.

Maybelle never married nor did she have children of her own. So, while the rest of the world doted on the great Lyla Fontaine and she on them, Maybelle's world revolved around sweet little Betts Knight who knew little of her father and only knew her mother as Lyla Fontaine, the absent actress.

When Momma was filming on site for her latest movie, Maybelle would take young Betts on their own great adventures. There was the zoo, the park and the beach, of course; but Betts's favorite outing was Sunday morning service at the Baptist Episcopal Missionary Church of South Los Angeles. The BEMC of South LA stood stately on the corner of 51st and Anaheim.

While the neighborhood was showing its years, the church was kept pristine and well-manicured. Pastor

James Overman was a stickler for exceptional first impressions. But it wasn't the building that young Betts grew to love; it was the church ladies, members of the Esther Circle, that hugged her and kissed her and made her feel like she belonged to each and every one of them. They treated her like their own. It seemed to Betts they were her fan club equivalent to the fans of Lyla Fontaine.

The women wore elaborate Sunday morning hats, the likes Betts had only seen in her momma's movies. She was fascinated by the array of colors and designs that matched each lady's dress; that matched her shoes; that matched her purse. Maybelle wore a pink chiffon cloche that sat atop her sleek black hair like a beautiful birthday gift with an oversized bow fastened to one side. Her feet overflowed the matching pink pumps and her floral muumuu swept about her with every step. Betts thought these ladies were stunning, far more glamorous than even the Hollywood friends of her mother.

Clarise Glover, an affectionate mother of the Baptist Episcopal Missionary Church and head of the Esther Circle, often wore a big brimmed black hat that nestled just above her eyes with a wide red ribbon adorned with clusters of geraniums wrapped around the crown. Precisely at the right moment, as the Spirit began to move, and the music began to swell, Mother Clarise would begin to sway to the rhythm. Betts could not take her eyes off her as she waited with excitement for the moment to unfold. From beneath that black hat with red ribbon and geraniums a hum would begin to rumble, followed by a deep throaty "Jeee-eee-suuuus," that rolled along like thunder building. The congregation would 'Uh huh" and "Amen" their approval of this move of the Spirit. Mother Clarise would then lift her hands in the air in response to their encouragement and continue the impromptu melody with something like, "Have mercy on us," or "Come quickly, Lord, to our rescue."

Pastor James would begin to break a sweat in his handsome, deep purple suit, crisp white shirt, and lavender striped tie. He would step to the pulpit, take his hanky from his coat pocket, and dab his forehead as he echoed back Mother Clarise's word from the Lord in song. That was the cue for the congregation to respond, the ladies would sway and dance, the men would clap their hands and eventually someone would need more room and make their way up the aisle to praise the Lord.

Betts loved the whole scene and as she watched, clinging to Maybelle's flower print dress, she would sometimes wonder why her momma wouldn't come with them when she was home. And, as she eyed Pastor James, she wondered if her daddy ever wore such a handsome purple suit.

It was there at the Baptist Episcopal Missionary Church of South Los Angeles that Betts, at the ripe old age of eleven, felt the Spirit move within her. Overcome by the soulful melody of Mother Clarise and the display of love by the congregants, Betts made her way to the altar one particularly bright, sunny, June morning and asked Jesus to come into her heart.

From the very first night Maybelle tucked the child into bed, she lavished Betts with Bible stories. Every morning Maybelle prayed with her as she readied for school. Maybelle Studer had prepared the heart of this Hollywood soul to understand how much God loved her and would never leave her alone. Even though her daddy had left, and her momma drove off time after time in a Porsche, Betts knew that Maybelle and Jesus would always be with her. So, there at that old oak altar, Betts knelt and pledged her life to Jesus as she prayed with Pastor James. Though his voice was gruff and loud she felt his emotion and heard the weeping and sniffling of the BEMC Esther Circle blessed to see this sweet little white girl become one of God's own.

It would be eleven years later, while Lyla Fontaine was filming in Paris, that Betts would dress in cap and gown for her graduation ceremony at Duke University. Crossing the stage with her Bachelor of Arts degree in Communication Studies in hand, Betts heard the quiet whisper of the Holy Spirit. She felt an ache deep in her soul, a longing to serve Christ. Dread mixed with the delight she was experiencing as she returned to her assigned seat and began to ponder her mother's reaction. It was possible Lyla would understand but more probable that she would spiral into dismay when she learned Betts would be primed for full-time ministry and a pulpit rather than meteorology and a greenscreen in graduate school.

As the ceremony was dismissed and graduates gathered with their families for pictures on the green, Betts found her cellphone and prepared to break the news to her mother. But there in her favorites list was Maybelle's number. Maybelle Studer answered immediately and wept as Betts announced the new direction her life would take. Through her tears, Maybelle shouted, "Praise Jeeesus!" After words of love and admiration were expressed and Betts promised to call again the coming week, Maybelle immediately called Mother Clarice and all the ladies of the Esther Circle of the Baptist Episcopal Missionary Church of South Los Angeles.

Betts had received a congratulatory call from her mother just prior to the commencement ceremony so she decided not to rush to talk with her again that day. Discussing her complete change of plans and life goals could wait. Instead, Betts spent the next few days packing up her apartment and exchanging goodbyes with roommates and friends. Two full days of preparation and line rehearsal passed before she dialed her mother's number to announce she would be pursuing a Master of Divinity degree with an emphasis on congregational leadership. And, of course, she had to leave a message on her mother's cell. Betts hung up the call after a brief description of the new plans for her future followed by an "I love you, Momma," and wondered if her mother would fully understand the impact the decision would have on their lives.

Two days later a FedEx envelope arrived with an airline ticket to Paris and a piece of lavender stationery folded neatly with it. "Let's talk, I'd like to know more." scrawled across it in Lyla's handwriting. I guess she understands, Betts thought as she rolled her eyes and sighed.

For Betts there was no argument against spending a summer in Paris before graduate school would begin in September. The argument, she feared, would come after the limousine driver escorted her to the front door of momma's rented twelve room French "cottage," as she referred to it. But low and behold, her mother greeted her with a hug and kisses on each cheek. Following the "I love yous," Lyla spoke words that eased Betts's anxious heart, "Why Betts, I had no idea, dear, that this 'Jesus thing' with you was so serious! I pledge to be your support, darling. You can rely on me to stand by your decision to move forward with your career. I'll, somehow, find a way to explain it to my colleagues in the business and ease them into the idea that you are going to pursue a religious life, hopefully they will understand as I do, love. It could be that they find it quite fashionable."

Hmmm...what direction will this guilt trip take? Betts wondered to herself.

However, Lyla's acceptance speech ended favorably, "No matter what you do, you have exceptional genes and an outstanding education, I'm sure you'll change the world..."

Betts listened to her mother's rehearsed approval and although she was sure a couple of her lines were crafted from movie scripts, which was expected, she was relieved there was no quarrel, not a word of discouragement spoken between them on the matter of Betts's "calling." Even so, as was the normal course of action, Betts would still take the next step into her future ridden with guilt. It was the gift her mother naturally bestowed upon her every move.

Chapter 2

Lyla Fontaine lived the Hollywood dream full of stage lights and glamor, diamonds and jewels until her wake-up call moment. At the age of 70 years, 3 days and 6.4 hours Lyla suffered a heart attack. Her left arm went numb, her back ached and she struggled to catch her breath as she pulled herself from her warm bath and struggled into her Linea Donatella nighty. She tried to call for her housekeeper, Angela, but couldn't summon enough air in her lungs to form much more than a whisper. She managed to reach her cell on the vanity to dial 911 and was thankful the call was traced to her home, being barely able to breathe an intelligible word to the dispatcher. The pain that gripped her chest was so severe she faded in and out of consciousness as the paramedics burst through her alarm system and found her on the bathroom floor.

Lyla was relieved, as any Hollywood star of her mature age would be, that she had found the strength to clothe herself and that Angela had laid out a designer nightgown that evening. She wrestled with the dreadful thought that she may have never forgiven God if the first responders had found her naked, especially at her age! The EMT's treated her with great respect and dignity, graciously granting her request as she eked out the words, "My lipstick, please." Angela, who had woken abruptly as the EMT's burst through the door, was at her side holding her hand and drew an appropriate lip shade for the hour and event before releasing Lyla into the full custody of the first responders. She was lifted onto a stretcher and whisked away to the Cedars-Sinai Emergency Room.

Betts managed to catch a red-eye flight to Los Angeles and remained at Lyla's side as she recovered in the hospital.

"Betts, dear, you live just too far from me," Lyla complained in a raspy voice when the endotracheal tube was removed. "Let me make arrangements for you to be at a church here on the west coast and not on the east coast thousands of miles away."

"Momma," Betts felt the guilt beginning to rise within her, "Why don't you come my way?" She suggested, "I mean, just for now, during your recovery."

"Oh, I could never put you out, I would be such a bother," Lyla said leading the guilt expedition into new territory. She had never really needed Betts before but found the guilt of inconvenience the natural path.

"But Momma, I can't leave my congregation for that long, you know that. Couldn't you please come to Florida and be near me and Auntie Beatrice," Betts continued noting that her mother was likely to respond to an element of begging.

Lyla assured Betts she would consider the temporary relocation as she drifted off to sleep. Lying alone in the ICU after midnight Lyla thought of calling on her dear friend and retired publicist, Beatrice Brown, who was currently residing at the Arcadia Retirement Village. Beatrice now referred to herself as Betty. Not that she had been especially famous, but her Hollywood influence occasionally followed her, and occasionally a gossip columnist would recognize her from her former glory days as publicist and assistant to the stars.

As Lyla's publicist, Beatrice had been called upon to conduct her fair share of interviews and walked many a Red Carpet at the side of her starlet friends and co-workers. But as the years swept by, she longed for a less stressful existence. She wondered if her golden years would be tarnished if she weren't able to come and go and enjoy life without meeting the demands of so many others. Beatrice Brown searched the remote ends of the earth for a community of contented, mature adults and stumbled on an internet website for a quaint little retirement village far from the hustle and bustle of Hollywood. In fact, it was far from the hustle and bustle of just about anything really. As she read through the promises of card club gatherings and cooking meals with other seniors in the Club House on Fridays, Beatrice could imagine her face on the website, looking comfortable and pleased. She pictured herself at a Monday evening Canasta table and boarding the Village People Mover for a day trip to some small hidden coastal shops and antique stores. In this setting she could go whenever the spirit moved and have lunch out with the girls every Thursday afternoon!

Beatrice, now content with the persona of Betty Brown, heard the report of Lyla's heart attack on the local 6:00 p.m. news and instinctively knew the call from Betts would be coming soon. It had been several years since Lyla Fontaine had made the headlines, so Betty perked up when she saw the caption under the local newscaster, "Lyla Fontaine hospitalized with heart problems."

Lyla, despite her age, proved her fame as WRXY TV out of Punta Gorda, Florida, 2629 miles east of Hollywood, broadcast her heart condition. Tears welled in Betty's eyes, but she smiled at her dear friend's renown. Sweet thoughts of Lyla filled her memory at the same moment worry gripped her chest but then, the twenty-something gal behind the reporter's desk announced that the *aging* star would remain hospitalized...!" Betty gasped and choked as her laughter turned to a snort. She had no idea what the reporter said next, thinking Lyla might have another heart episode if she were to hear reports claiming the name Lyla Fontaine as an "aging star!"

But the gravity of the news report prepared Betty for the call from Betts. That was the routine. Betty never called first, she waited. Despite her retirement, she remained one of Lyla's closest confidants and she knew that a report of Lyla's health and instructions for the next step would come to her first, before anyone else. That had been the routine for over fifty-five years.

Betts's call brought relief to Betty. She was thrilled to hear that the doctors expected a complete recovery, the good report relieved Betty of her guilt of giggling at Lyla's "aging" expense, but the heart attack shook Lyla. She took the cell phone from her daughter, "Dear One," She let her words roll off her tongue like sweet honey. Lyla learned early in Hollywood that a savory presentation of a new opportunity was critical. "Would you mind if I took a small holiday and came for a visit? I've had a bit of an episode, nothing to worry about, really. I just need, so badly, to get away from the traffic and ruckus of the city. May I spend a week or two in the Village with you? I'm afraid I just need to breathe, Beatrice, and I can't do that in Hollywood." Lyla believed her appeal to her publicist was dramatic, yet sincere, however, to clinch the deal she added, "I must also confess, that the thought of recovering with anyone but you and Betts nearby, seems just dreadful."

Lyla sounded tired, Betty thought, maybe Ms. Twenty-Something, the reporter, had been right in her description after all. She wanted to give in, fling wide her little cottage door and welcome her friend with open arms, but unfortunately there was a "but!" After all, Betty had stayed hidden for four and half years in "the Village" as Lyla had so eloquently called it. "Lyla, I'd love to have you..."

"Oh, thank you dear, I knew I could depend on you, as always. It's settled then, Beatrice, I'll be on my way sometime next..." Lyla interjected before Betty could finish her thought.

Betty, however, after years as Lyla's publicist, knew how to accommodate the star but on her own terms, "Wait a minute, Lyla dear! Not so fast, it's really not settled, not just yet!"

From two thousand miles Betty heard Lyla's deep, tired sigh through her cell, "Beatrice? You don't want me, love?" Both Betts and Betty were recipients of Lyla's masterful art of employing guilt with very few words.

"Lyla, yes, I'd love to have you BUT, I don't want Arcadia Village to turn into a tourist hot-spot, dear, and you know that YOU would cause a media onslaught! Face it, you attract the crowds. You always have and always will. Now listen to me, you need to understand that I have kept a low profile. No one here knows who I was or what I did all my life and I don't want them to catch on now. I've spent four years shedding my past and I love the life I'm living, and are you listening, Lyla? I can do so because, I guess you could say, because I'm living undercover. I've gone incognito! I so enjoy the ease of coming and going when and where I want. I drive myself, love! I don't have a door man or an office or anyone who checks up on me! And my phone hardly ever rings. It's a dream come true. Get this, Lyla, on occasion, I even cook! If, and I am stressing to you if you come here, you cannot come as Lyla Fontaine and you cannot call me Beatrice. You cannot sputter words of disbelief when I exchange recipes or go to my canasta club. Do you understand, Lyla? I am not Beatrice and you, dear, cannot live here, with me or near me, as Lyla Fontaine. I am Betty Brown, now."

Betty? Oh, what a dreadful name, totally devoid of character and presence, Lyla grumbled to herself. Feeling somewhat overwhelmed by the lack of charm in her friend's newly chosen name and the effort it took to keep up with the conversation, Lyla expressed her love to Beatrice and told her she would consider her kind request that she come and stay.

Betty hung up smiling. She had briefly thought of reminding Lyla that it had been her request to visit the Retirement Village, not vice versa but Betty bit her tongue. Lyla would never change; she had the uncanny ability or maybe it was even a gift, to believe every situation was crafted for her own favor.

Lyla sent Betts back to the mansion for a restful night knowing Angela would be there to care for her. Lying alone listening to the shushing of the hospital equipment, she had time to consider Beatrice's new lifestyle. Lyla was intrigued with the idea of coming and going as she pleased and living life in anonymity. Maybe it would be the prescription she needed, without the cooking part, of course. She pictured herself buying one of the cute little cars she had ridden in while filming one of her movies in Paris. She could drive it where she wanted, whenever she wanted.

The idea of freedom from the pressures and stress of paparazzi and social engagements for a few weeks intrigued Lyla Fontaine. *Beatrice, or Betty, as she now preferred, may have a great, new plot in which to live life. Lyla began to dream this could be my great comeback.* Her eyes sparked new life; *I will play the role of myself!* With that she was jolted with an awareness like a bolt of lightning from the heavens, *this is my encore!*

A nursing assistant entered her room to note her vitals printing out on a long piece of paper falling to the floor. Lyla reached for the young woman's hand, "This might be the greatest role I ever play!"

"You bet honey," the woman answered, thinking Lyla Fontaine was still delirious under the influence of anesthesia.

The next morning Betts peeked around the door into Lyla's hospital room not wanting to wake her convalescing mother. Lyla was sitting up, wide wake, long grey curls combed and pulled back in a ponytail, "Get Beatrice on the phone, Betts, and please make arrangements for me to fly to Arcadia."

Betty's cell buzzed on her nightstand, "Good morning dear, this is Lyla of course, but you can call me Anne, my name will once again be Anne Knight. And Anne is on her way to visit you at the Arcadia Retirement Village. Betts will make the arrangements, and no one will know but you and me and Betts. This will be our secret. We'll stay under wraps and the rest of the world will believe that Lyla Fontaine is recovering nicely in her Beverly Hills mansion."

Betty heard life returning to Lyla Fontaine's voice.

The conversation ended with Betty listening as Betts questioned her mother, "Are you sure, Momma? This is not the life you are accustomed to living. You won't have 6500 square feet or a private pool or Delia's Boutique to fit you. In fact, Momma, you won't have any need to be fitted, there won't be evening dinner parties or premiers, you know."

But Lyla, now Anne, had made up her mind and both Betty and Betts knew there would be no budging her, heart episode or not! Betts made the arrangements to fly "Anne Knight" by private jet to a small local airport where she would be met by Betty Brown and whisked off to the Arcadia Retirement Village anonymously. After securing her mother on a private flight, Betts would fly to New Smyrna Beach commercially and drive to meet them both. Once Momma was tucked away and hidden in the Village, Betts would return to her congregation and get back to her first love, the Wesley United Methodist Church of New Smyrna Beach, Florida.

Chapter 3

Smith Kennedy stabled himself as he climbed from the wheelchair that transported him from room 301 to the Highlander. Leaving Florida Hospital Orlando, Smith was giving his son, Johnson, the silent treatment. He had spent the last few weeks thanking God for seeing him through the stroke, but Smith was not the least bit happy contemplating physical therapy in Naples and living with Johnson for the next three months. Not that he minded spending time with his son, he often visited him at his home, but this stroke had put a damper on his plans for developing a new golf course and continuing his behind the scenes involvement of the senior tour of the PGA.

Smith was a young 73 years old; he ate healthy and kept active and fit. This stroke, or as the doctors referred to it at Florida Hospital, brain attack, sent him on a tailspin. All he could remember of the first hours following the incident was the beep of the infusion pump emptying its medicine into his veins while he lay in the ICU. Now, leaving the hospital, his short-term memory remained a mixed-up jumble of emotion and thought, rolling around inside his head just out of reach. He felt as if he needed a mental lasso to pull his intellect back to the frontal lobe of his brain where his thoughts could be categorized and ordered. Doctors, nurses, and physical therapists bombarded him with questions he knew the answers to but somehow, they were drifting, somewhere in his memory, making every response sluggish and troubling. When the words would finally come, they moved from brain to mouth in slow motion.

But Smith was determined and fought hard to find the memories he knew he needed to fully recover; the memories that were the root to becoming the old Smith Kennedy once again. Alone in the hospital, he spoke his thoughts out loud so he could hear what he was saying. Hearing his memories resonating between the four walls of his small room helped solidify the events that had taken place in his life: marriage, winning the Masters Tournament, the birth of his son. The stroke would now be added to that list as it quickly became apparent it would change his life forever. Working hard to open the fist of his right hand, Smith realized it would be his choice how well he would survive; he could either fight back through physical therapy or resign to talking about golf rather than playing.

The days in the hospital rolled one into another. He chose to fight to regain the complete use of his left hand and arm, but his body wasn't responding to his liking. Although the doctors assured him, with hard work, he would regain a "good portion" of mobility, a "good portion" was not good enough!

It was a bright January afternoon that Smith was released from the hospital. He maneuvered his way into the passenger seat of his son's black Highlander and Johnson chauffeured his father down the Florida interstate towards Naples. Johnson made the decision that his father would come to Naples for physical therapy and Smith had reluctantly agreed.

As they drove the familiar route, Smith began to focus his thoughts on what would be coming around the next bend. He tested his brain and memory every chance he could, but the interstate signs blended one into another. He became frustrated trying to make sense of the green exit signs coming into focus then disappearing overhead. But as the Highlander left the four-lane interstate for Florida Highway 17 his memory was jolted. Recollections of driving Highway 17 from Orlando to Naples began to become sharper. The fog that had settled in his brain was beginning to lift ever so slightly as sights along the road evoked memories of Claire. His heart ached as he thought of her.

He and Claire had settled in Orlando eighteen years before she lost her battle with cancer. Since then, he'd kept Orlando as home base while he traveled the world with the Professional Golfers Association, consulting with golf course owners, and playing the game with presidents, kings and even a few dictators. In his dealings, golf spoke a universal language. The greatest deals between corporations or nations were negotiated on a golf course, somewhere, and Smith had had the opportunity to be an integral part of many historical moments.

But after Claire's death, when he was home, the house echoed with emptiness and silence. When the loneliness began to ring too loudly, rather than allow himself to become enmeshed in Claire's memory, Smith would drive to Naples and spend time with their son. The trip had been taken less frequently in recent years, it had been twelve years since Claire's passing, but the trek on Highway 17, through ranch lands and orange groves, away from the clamor of the coast was always a welcomed trip.

As he watched the road signs along the two-lane, Smith searched his memory pulling up data about what town would be at the next turn. He tried to remember the names of the rivers they would cross, and which tourist spot would be coming into view. As Johnson rambled on about how great life would be as two old bachelors, Smith tuned him out bringing his brain into submission.

He felt a flicker of hope within himself as they passed the OK Gas Station and Convenience Store in Wauchula. He recalled stopping there several times to get a cup of really bad coffee that kept him awake and alert on the winding road.

And then, to his delight, he remembered Zolfo Springs would be the next burgh along the road. He hadn't found anything of much interest there over the years and never slowed beyond the speed limit at the four corners that marked the Zolfo Springs Historic District, but if his memory served him, there was a dreary trailer park with a wrought-iron welcome sign hanging between two steel posts at the entrance. His memory jogged old forgotten feelings of despair for the people who lived there. It didn't seem to him to be the kind of place that someone would aspire to move to and live out their golden years. He had often thought he should do something for the folks that settled there but soon after he had driven past, and the place was out of sight, it was out of mind, until the next trip through.

And there it was ahead, just as he had forced his brain to remember. Now as a passenger, Smith had the opportunity to look a little closer; the sign hung with a slight tilt and he read the words still legible:

Vintage Lane Trailer and Mobile Home Park
No Speeding!

The whole scene left him feeling rather sad. He made a mental note to try to remember this place. Why? He wasn't exactly sure, but he would remember Vintage Lane for a stop in the future, when he would be the driver, not the passenger.

Memories trickled into his thoughts and Smith realized that Arcadia would be the next town Johnson would chauffeur him through. He reminisced of the days that he and Claire would stop and stroll through the quaint antique shops just off the main highway. They would walk arm-in-arm along Maple Street and peek inside the dusty "junk" stores as he referred to them. Claire loved the hunt for something unique, an antique knick-knack that Smith would consider useless and obnoxious. Not Claire, though, she would give the relic as a thoughtful gift to an unsuspecting recipient who would undoubtedly receive it with tears and hugs and accolades of thanksgiving. After Claire was laid to rest in Chapel Hill Cemetery, Smith never stopped again.

Rounding the bend, Highway 17 left behind the orange groves and ranches to merge for a short distance with Highway 70. The Highlander by-passed the side roads and the antique alleyways. Entering the

Arcadia city limits Smith caught sight of a spot he had completely forgotten. Even if he hadn't had a stroke, he probably would never have remembered it, but there ahead was Putt-Putt Golf. Claire had often suggested that he invest in Putt-Putt. While golf was known as the rich man's sport, she would always spout that Putt-Putt made golf available to families with little ones and teens on their first date. She often reminded him with great excitement that vacationers loved to play Putt-Putt. Smith would always smile at Claire's naivety and dismiss the idea immediately.

As they drove closer, a traffic light ahead turned red. Johnson slowed the Highlander to a stop which gave Smith the opportunity to take a good hard look at the aging business. Then he saw it, there beneath the Putt-Putt sign was a 4x8 piece of plywood with the hand-painted words, "Going Out of Business – For Sale by Owner."

"Stop!" was the only word Smith's brain could lasso and release from his mouth. "Stop!"

"Holy smokes, Dad, you trying to give ME a stroke? I am already stopped!" Johnson huffed back.

"No...wait!" The words came slowly as Johnson paused and waited for the light to turn green. Smith pointed, "Stop there!"

Smith was so excited that his brain had formed a new idea in the spur of a moment that he could hardly speak. He struggled to voice the words he needed to say. He wanted Johnson to stop at the Putt-Putt so that he could inquire about the sale of the business. He wanted to buy the Putt-Putt Golf that was right down the road from the old antique shops that Claire had loved so dearly and he wanted to engage in his own physical therapy there on the Putt-Putt golf course. But those words weren't readily available in his excitement, so he simply pointed to the miniature golf course and said, "Stop there!"

"What? What are you talking about, Dad? Stop where? Are you alright? Do you need to use the bathroom?" Johnson's trail of questions frustrated Smith even more.

Smith huffed loudly, he had been enjoying giving Johnson the silent treatment and now he was beginning to understand why. "Stop at the Putt-Putt...I'm going to buy it."

"Holy cow, that stroke made you nuts, Dad! NO, I'm not going to stop so you can buy a Putt-Putt Golf Course. Are you kidding me?"

"Johnson, stop there, NOW!" Smith said in a low, firm voice. "Stop while you can help me make this happen," the light turned green, "or I'll come back in an Uber and do it myself."

Johnson knew to trust his dad's words. If Smith Kennedy wanted to purchase a Putt-Putt Golf Course, stroke or not, he would find a way to do it. He pulled into the parking lot of a small diner on the opposite side of Highway 70.

"Okay Dad, listen, let's go in here, have a cup of coffee and talk about this. I'm not sure you're thinking sensibly or if this is an effect of the stroke, okay?"

Smith agreed. Although he hated to admit it, Johnson had made a reasonable request. While they sipped a cup of coffee, he would wrangle his thoughts and words to the best of his ability and express the ideas that were forming in his mind. He knew Johnson was a good son, looking out for his father. He deserved the respect owed him for his help in this situation. However, Smith had made up his mind and was going to buy the Putt-Putt Golf Course and work through his own PT program whether Johnson was in favor or not!

Many times, in and around a golf course it was not unusual for people to recognize Smith Kennedy but now that his glory days had long since passed, outside of the golf world people often missed the opportunity to acknowledge one of the greatest players in history. Two-time winner of the Masters Tournament, Smith had been called upon to be the spokesman for a myriad of sponsors from golf equipment to breakfast cereal, the man was a multimillionaire many times over. Thankfully, this was one of those moments that Smith Kennedy was not recognized.

The teenage waitress sashayed over to the table, popped her gum before addressing the men, "Can I get ya somethin'?" Johnson asked for two cups of black decaf. They had taken a table at the window with the Putt-Putt in clear view across the street. When the waitress returned with their coffee, Smith slowly and deliberately asked her, "Do many folks play Putt-Putt over there?"

"Friday and Saturday nights get a good crowd, but the place goes crazy in March when all the cowboys are in town for the rodeo."

"The rodeo?" Smith and Johnson knew nothing of a rodeo in Arcadia.

"Oh man," the waitress snapped her gum and continued, "It's just like the Wild West around here in March. The cowboys and cowgirls come from all over the country to compete in The All Florida Rodeo Championship and we're bustin' at the seams when folks come from everywhere to watch. The Diner packs 'em in all day and the Putt-Putt stays open till at least midnight. It's a blast! Can't believe ya never heard about it. Where y'all from anyway? I'm just hopin' the Putt-Putt's still open during rodeo week. The place is up for sale." The waitess hardly drew a breath as she rattled on. She looked right at Smith, "You oughta buy the place, mister. You buy it and I'll help y'all out." The young waitress giggled at her suggestion, but Smith noted the moment as a sign from God, Himself.

"Yup, you buy it and I'll help ya!" She repeated but that didn't stop her from concluding her thoughts out loud. "You'll need my help and I only work here a couple a hours after school to fill in. Why don't ya hire me and we'll team up and maybe I'll lasso a cowboy come rodeo week!" she finished with a gasp and smile.

The name tag on the waitress's apron read: TRAINEE. "Well, listen Miss Trainee," Smith said with a little more life in his words.

She giggled again and with renewed breath blurted, "Oh mister you make me laugh! My name idn't Trainee, I'm Crystal and believe it or not, my last name is Bell. Can you believe that my momma and my daddy named me Crystal Bell?"

Smith looked at his son, Johnson Kennedy, who was born and named on election day. With the last name of Kennedy, the only logical choice for a first name would be to celebrate one of the great presidential tickets elected to office, thus Smith and Claire christened their infant with two last names: Johnson Kennedy. "Nope, I can hardly believe a momma and daddy would do such a thing to their child, Miss Bell!" Smith's words rolled slowly out from behind his smile as he looked at the scowl on Johnson's face. Realizing Johnson would never truly forgive him for his name made Smith feel a little bit proud. He had achieved greatness as a father; he had eternally embarrassed his son!

Smith continued his conversation, "Miss Crystal Bell, if I should purchase the Putt-Putt Golf Course, I would be honored if you would consent to be my first employee. Keep watch, and if that For Sale sign comes down, you come look for me, okay?"

"You got it, boss," she said with a wink. She had no idea that she had just cut a deal with one of the wealthiest men in sports.

Johnson, stiffened, he wasn't exactly primed to see his dad sign on the bottom line of a sale agreement, but he had noticed that his father's demeanor had completely changed during the course of the short conversation with Miss Crystal Bell. He watched his father's shoulders drop and relax, he used his left hand without even realizing as he reached for a spoon to stir some cream into the overpowering black coffee, but most importantly, his eyes regained their twinkle. Life was returning to the man.

"Okay, Dad, let's just say you buy the place, you practice putting there and you actually show some signs of successful physical therapy. That is all well and good, but are you going to hire a driver to bring you up from Naples a couple of times a week? I mean, really Dad, take a minute and consider this logically, okay?

You don't live anywhere near here. How about we look for something closer to Naples?"

Smith raised a hand, showing Johnson his palm in father-like fashion, "Johnson." He began slowly but his words grew stronger and his voice firm, "I understand your concern son but,"

"But? But what, Dad?"

Smith continued, "I'm 73 years old and if God is going to take me home, He'll take me in Naples just as easily as Arcadia. I need to do this. You know as well as I do that, I'll last about three hours in Naples before I need to find a project to get my mind engaged and working. Now, consider this; I can refurbish that little Putt-Putt Golf Course across the street, or I can refurbish your basement, bathrooms, and patio, which do you prefer I make my next project?"

Johnson kept up the protest knowing that he was on the losing side of this battle, "But Dad, where will you live? Who will see that you're taken care of? Who will cook?"

As the conversation persisted, Smith moved his eyes from the Putt-Putt Course and scanned Highway 70 trying to formulate a plan. He had made up his mind that he would buy the place, but he wanted to make a fair attempt at convincing Johnson that all would be well. Smith thought to himself, *I'm a man of faith, for goodness sake, there is a mission here somewhere.* He struggled for a strategy to work through the details and keep Johnson's worrying at bay. *Lord, could you help me with this one?* he prayed silently.

Chapter 4

Money was not a hindrance and Smith had always had a good business sense as well, but he knew Johnson was concerned with the effects the stroke may have had on his decision-making process. He could hire help; he could hire a cook and a driver and everything else he might need. As Johnson was carrying on about the whole world taking advantage of Smith in his "situation," Smith spotted a neatly kept drive with tidy flower beds, trimmed hedges inside a four foot stucco wall and a replica of the Venus De Milo wearing a scarf and stocking cap. He squinted to be sure he was seeing her correctly and then he noticed an aqua-marine welcome sign shaped like a giant seashell. Engraved in the sign just below "Welcome" Smith read

"Arcadia Retirement Village
Active retirement living for seniors on the go!"

"I'll live right there, Johnson." Smith pointed out the window, "Do you see the sign for that retirement village? And there are a couple of golf carts on a cart path, son. I think it's paved along the stucco wall. Do you see it along the highway?" Smith pointed across Highway 70 and followed the path with his eyes. "Hey! Would you look at that! It runs right past the Piggly Wiggly and, well, I think that's a little restaurant over there. I think it may be paved past the Putt-Putt Golf Course. I wouldn't need a driver if I could get there by golf cart."

Slowly and steadily Smith kept talking even though Johnson tried to cut him off, "Looks like the good Lord has found a home for me, Johnson. A home and grocery store and a place to eat and my own physical therapy gig, right here all in about a half of a mile that I can maneuver with a golf cart. I've got a few of those, you know."

Johnson tried to protest again but Smith continued, "Now top that with any argument you want, but when you're done I'm going to have you drive me over to cut a deal with the owner of the Putt-Putt then I'm going to have you stop at the Arcadia Retirement Village to find a little place to rent. Then, and only then, can you take me to Naples so I can pick up a few things I'll need, including a golf cart, before I move in here." As he finished this lengthy thought, Smith silently thanked the Lord for helping him. He not only had blessed Smith with the ability to have that thought, it was a rather inventive thought, too!

Smith called Crystal Bell over to the table and handed her the biggest tip she would ever get at the diner. While he and Johnson were having their discussion, he had neatly folded a one-hundred-dollar bill so the numbers were concealed when he put it in her hand. Folding it had taken a few minutes longer than it would have in his pre-stroke life, but he was pleased he managed the fine motor skills post-stroke. "You keep your eyes on that sign Miss Bell, I'll be looking for good help over there and I think I would like to put you on the payroll. Who knows, maybe we can find you a cowboy this March," he said with a wink. She giggled as the two men headed out the door.

They had barely gotten off the sidewalk and into the parking lot when Crystal charged through the diner door yelling, "Mister, Hey mister! Wait! Y'all must-a made a mistake!" She pushed the crinkled bill into his hand.

"Nope, not at all, Miss Bell, I didn't make a mistake and your honesty just proved you to be an honest asset to my new Putt-Putt business."

She gave Smith a puzzled look and he explained, "I knew when you opened that bill and saw the amount you would have two options; if you were an ordinary teenager you would probably keep it to yourself thinking my mistake was your gain. But if you were an extraordinary teenager you would try your best to make sure the mistake was rectified. Crystal Bell, you are an extraordinary young lady, and should I purchase the business across the street, I would like to make you a junior manager of the Arcadia Putt-Putt Golf Course. You watch for that sign to come down, I'm counting on you."

Johnson looked at his father in amazement. Smith understood. Just earlier today he was having trouble pulling any thoughts and ideas in his head together and now he was more rational than he had ever been.

Crystal gasped. "Listen Mister, I don't even know your name or nothin' about ya but I'll be happy as a clam to work for ya! Don't you want your hundred dollars back? I didn't do nothin' but pour ya a cup of coffee and the diner coffee just idn't that good!"

"My name's Smith Kennedy. You earned the hundred by being honest, keep it, but don't let me down, I may want you to come to work for me in a couple of weeks." Smith scrawled his phone number on a scrap of paper he found in the Highlander and he handed it to the teen.

"No way! You're the best boss ever and I haven't even set foot on the job, yet! Thanks for the tip." She waved good-bye and danced a little two-step on her way back into the diner. She stopped at the door, turned with a twirl and yelled to Smith, "Hey boss, get that sign up soon!" In the diner she tucked the bill in her apron, "Hey, you guys know any rich folks around here with two last names? That guy was Jones Smith or something like that, ring a bell?" No one had any idea what she was talking about.

Seated in the car Johnson turned to his father, "Dad, I know you want to do this and I'll help you because I know you're going to do this, but may I make one very strong suggestion?"

Smith knew he would need to acquiesce to Johnson's suggestion to ease his mind, "Yes, I will listen and take into consideration anything you have to say, son."

"You're getting stronger, and your excitement about this project seems to help you focus. I watched you use your left hand and you didn't even think about it, you just did it. I heard that whole spiel you rolled out to Crystal. It was remarkable. I know this project is going to help you heal quickly. But, Dad, could I suggest that you keep a low profile."

Johnson explained, "Your focus, although it has improved remarkably today, is still a bit foggy, I am concerned that someone may take advantage of you. Right now, you may not be so quick to notice a fraud or a swindler. You attract attention with your name and prominence, and there's no avoiding that, am I right?"

Smith sighed and shook his head in agreement.

"So, what would you think, just for safety's sake, if you could live here sort of, well, incognito? The good folks of Arcadia don't really need to know who you are, do they? I mean, just until we're sure your thought process is totally back on track."

Smith hated the idea that his son might be right. Not so much because he wasn't completely well; mind, soul and body, but more so because he was right about the culture. As they pulled the car into the Putt-Putt he agreed. "Okay, I'll use my middle name, Leonard, just call me Leonard Smith."

Offering cash at the Putt-Putt made for an exceptionally smooth deal. Although the owner was willing to settle at much less than asking price, he, Johnson and Smith, who signed the agreement papers Leonard Smith, all knew it was still more than the place was actually worth.

The next stop was the Arcadia Retirement Village. The Highlander wound its way past the Venus De Milo and giant seashell. Neither Johnson nor Smith made a remark about the naked statue wearing a winter cap. They followed the sign pointing the direction to the Arcadia Retirement Village Office.

Herbert Lewis looked up from his desk as the men stepped out of the bright sunlight and into the air-conditioned building. He stood to meet the men with an outstretched hand, his manager pin secured to his lapel. "Hello and welcome to the Village. What can I do for you gentlemen today?" Herb was eyeing Smith, he raised an eyebrow causing his forehead to furrow, "Do I know you? Have you been here before?"

"Nope, but you wouldn't believe how much I get that. I must have one of those faces, you know what I mean?" Smith chortled.

"No, no, I know you. How do I know you? Have I seen you on TV? I have, haven't I? Why, you've been in commercials. That's it! I saw you in an electric razor commercial at Christmas time a few years ago."

Oh, for Pete's sake, Smith thought, *I've won the Masters, I've travelled the globe and the man remembers me in a razor commercial.* He wanted to pop the guy in the nose but instead forced a smile and nodded.

Johnson stepped in, "Yup, that's my dad, you've seen him in a lot of commercials over the years, but he would really like to keep that under wraps, you know what I mean? He'd like to settle into a nice quiet little village like this and just live a peaceful life, live incognito away from the paparazzi. The commercial paparazzi."

Johnson glanced down at the man's name tag, "Herb, can I call you Herb? The commercial paparazzi are relentless. They have made my dad's life miserable." Smith thought Johnson was pouring it on a bit thick, but Herb seemed to hang on every word. For greater effect, Johnson lowered his voice to a whisper, "Do you have a little place that my dad, Leonard, can rent for a while to get away from the constant barrage of his fans? When he signed up to do commercials, he never realized the following he would have!"

Herb blinked, "Believe it or not, you're not the first to come here for those reasons."

Johnson wondered what Herb meant by that remark.

"We here at the Arcadia Retirement Village will do all we can to keep your or shall I say 'our' little secret safe. And Leonard," Herb draped his arm over Smith's shoulders, "I have just the place for you! Let me show you a little furnished bungalow that just became vacant. The owners have decided to move back with their children for the time being but didn't want to put the place up for sale just yet. Let's head over to Sunset Lane, you're going to like this spot."

The men elected to take Johnson's car and drove the winding lanes through the Village following Herb's directions from the back seat. Smith wasn't especially concerned with what it looked like; he was beginning to feel tired from all the events of the day. He just wanted to sign the papers but played along, pretending to be interested and even managed a few "Ooo's" and "Ahh's" during his guided tour of the ocean blue, four-room cottage.

Herb thought ahead and brought all the appropriate paperwork with him in his briefcase. When Smith signed on the spot, using the name Leonard and pulled three month's rent, in cash, from his pocket, Herb took a double-take and made a remark about how lucrative it must be to make commercials.

"You have no idea, Herb, you have no idea," Johnson said as he shook his head, "But remember, this is hush-hush. Let's keep my dad, the 'king of commercials,' our little secret."

"Yes, sir, of course."

As Johnson backed the Highlander out onto Sunset Lane, Smith caught sight of a strikingly beautiful woman signing papers on her front porch as a polished, sporty silver Porsche was being parked in her carport. She looked up from atop the three steps of the pink cottage and flashed a smile that made Smith blink and catch his breath. With that, she waved and disappeared behind the front door. He wasn't sure what caught his attention first, the classic car or the exceptionally, attractive woman. As he turned the doorknob and pushed open his front door two thoughts flooded Smith's brain: why was there a silver Porsche at the Arcadia Retirement Village and why did that woman look so dog-gone familiar?

Chapter 5

Betts was looking forward to the two-hour drive home as she pulled from her mother's cottage onto Sunset Lane and made her way out of the Village. She was pleasantly surprised at her mother's willingness to spend a month or so in Arcadia Retirement Village and quite relieved that Lyla made the decision to revive Anne Knight. A few weeks of recovery with Auntie Beatrice in the peaceful surroundings of the Village, would be good for Lyla's healing; however, knowing her mother, Betts wasn't sure how long the peace would last. For now, though, she was hidden in Arcadia, Florida only a short drive away rather than a cross country flight. Betts raised her shoulders and breathed a long sigh of relief as she headed for Highway 70 North passing the Venus De Milo and the seashell-shaped, aqua-marine Welcome sign that bid *Good-Bye and Please Drive Safely* at the park exit.

Anne left her Beverly Hills home in the care of Angela, the housekeeper, and a grounds man who were instructed to move cars and turn on lights convincing curious tourists and paparazzi that Lyla Fontaine was securely convalescing inside her mansion behind the iron gate. Her mail would be sent in sealed envelopes to Betts, never forwarded and all calls would be directed to her assistant, Judy, as had been done since Auntie Beatrice had retired. Judy worked for Lyla under strict privacy rules so there would be nothing unordinary if anyone in the industry would try to reach her.

As Betts moved into traffic, she turned her attention to the modest diner in the Acadia Plaza across the street. Wondering if Crystal Bell would be serving, she decided to stop in for a coffee-to-go and tell the young waitress she would be back in town in a few weeks. Crystal seemed to be an old soul, insightful for her age, always smiling and encouraging the elder clients in the diner. Betts and Anne had stopped in one afternoon for a lunch salad and Crystal carried on "oohing" and "aahing" over Anne's beauty. "Ma'am, you could be in the movies," she belted out as she delivered their table settings.

Of course, taking the opportunity to ooze her passion for drama within her, Lyla portrayed her role as Anne Knight flawlessly, "Oh, you are much too kind, you sweet little thing. I admit, I have lived a rather charmed life but I'm afraid far too many years have passed by for me to take the Hollywood path now, dear."

Crystal carried on, "Pardon me for sayin' lady, but you even sound like a sophisticated Hollywood actress. You sure missed yer calling!"

Betts jumped into the dialogue unsure how her mother might respond to the gush of admiration flowing from the young woman, "Your name tag says 'Trainee,' darling, what is your name, really?"

"I'm Crystal and believe it or not, my last name is Bell. Can you believe that my momma and my daddy named me Crystal Bell?" She spouted the same spiel to everyone who asked her name.

"Well, Crystal, my mother has just moved into the Arcadia Retirement Village across the street and I'll be heading back to New Smyrna Beach in a few days." Betts pointed to Anne and then to the Village across the parking lot and four lanes of traffic. "We're mother and daughter, enjoying a nice quiet life, no fuss or bother..." Betts wasn't confident in her mother's new found identity and hoped to stress to chatty Crystal that there was nothing out of the ordinary about the two of them when Crystal interrupted.

Looking at Anne she interjected, "Ma'am, if you're gonna be here in Arcadia," then turning her attention to Betts, "And Ma'am, if you're gonna be in New Smyrna Beach, let me give ya my phone number. I'm always happy to run some errands and do some shoppin'! I just love helping and I'm honest. Honest!" she giggled.

Anne was moved by the kindness of the girl, "You are a delight, Crystal, much like my Betts, when she was your age. It would be an honor to have your phone number and have you assist me as I need. Thank you, dear. I will gladly pay you handsomely for your kindness."

Crystal jumped back and contorted her face into an exaggerated surprised look, "Ma'am!" she exclaimed, "I don't charge the folks in the Village to run their errands! My goodness! I just live down the road here. We, ma'am, are neighbors and neighbors just help each other." She scribbled her name and number on a napkin and shoved it in Anne's direction, "Just gimme a call when you need somethin'!"

A tear welled in the corner of Anne's eye. She was overwhelmed with the child's offer of kindness. The two ladies tipped Crystal Bell generously before they left. Anne hadn't known many people in her life as Lyla Fontaine who simply liked her for who she was and did kind things for her just because they were neighbors.

As Betts started her return trip to New Smyrna Beach, she pulled into the diner's parking area and found a slot next to a shiny black Highlander close to the door. She stopped in the doorway as she left the bright light of the morning to refocus in the shadows of the air-conditioned room. While Crystal was busy, flitting table to table, Betts leaned against the counter waiting for the opportunity to get the girl's attention and order her usual coffee to-go. "No sugar and just enough cream to make it look pretty, please," she would remind Crystal. Betts blinked but was sure she had seen a set of wings on the back of this little guardian angel who, she was sure was sent by God, to watch over her mother. Between Auntie Beatrice and Crystal, Betts imagined she might even be able to sleep at night!

While she waited, Crystal swung through the room with a coffee pot and landed at a table of two men beside a big window; the older gentleman looked vaguely familiar and was seated across from a younger man who appeared to be his son. Betts imagined they were likely living out circumstances similar to her and her mother. She premised that the older man was probably a resident of the Village and the younger man was visiting; making his weekly check and treating his father to a leisurely lunch before he started his return trip home. Betts envied the younger man for not having to worry about a famous, wealthy, world-renowned parent. *Oh, for that pleasure, Lord. Forgive my envy but I do wish Momma and I could live as simple a life as the two of them,* Betts secretly prayed.

Betts traded Crystal her business card for the to-go cup. She rattled off instructions to call if any health situations were to come up with Anne. After repeating herself several times like a first-time mother to a teenage babysitter, the order for the two men at the table was called up from the kitchen. Betts hugged Crystal goodbye and thanked her one more time on her way out the door. As she looked back at the diner, she noticed the two men pointing out the window at the dreadful looking Putt-Putt across the street and hoped they were talking about tearing it down. What an eyesore it was in this tidy little town.

The drive home was uneventful, just as Betts liked it. It gave her plenty of time to run through the upcoming Sunday morning sermon she had prepared for her congregation. When she arrived in New Smyrna, Betts's first stop was, of course, the church. It was early afternoon so she hoped that Ruth White, her administrative assistant would still be in the office. She pulled into the parking spot marked with the sign PASTOR and Ruth's maroon SUV loaded with car seats, cat food, and little sticky things clinging between the seats was parked across the lot. Vinyl stick-figures of dad, mom, three children of all sizes and two cats clung to the rear window.

Ruth was a wonderful assistant and had been the first to welcome Rev. Betts Knight to the Wesley United Methodist Church with open arms when she was appointed there five years prior to her mother's heart episode.

"HEY! You're back and right on time, Pastor!" Ruth's voice rang out as Betts walked in the door. "So, first let me ask you, 'how's your momma?' then I'll get into the nitty gritty of who's where and who's done what since you've been gone."

Betts gave all the details of getting her mother moved and her belongings settled into the Arcadia Retirement Village with her dear friend, Betty. However, just as the last suitcase of shoes was pulled through the door of Betty's bright yellow bungalow, a "for rent by owner" sign appeared in the window of a pink cottage directly across the street. From behind one of the piles of boxes the movers were just beginning to unpack came her mother's voice, "Take me to see that nice gentleman in the Village office, will you dear? You know I love Beatrice to the moon and back but, I think I'd like to stay in my own space in that adorable pink cottage across the Lane."

Betts explained to Ruth that it was at that precise moment, two days ago, when she placed the call to the church board president requesting to extend her stay in Arcadia, allowing her to get Lyla resettled across the street on Sunset Lane. She continued with a confession to Ruth that she and her mother were able to convince Herb Lewis, manager of the Arcadia Retirement Village, that Anne Knight had at one time been a stand in and double for the great Lyla Fontaine. He schmoozed Momma telling her that he could see the resemblance, but Anne looked years younger than Lyla Fontaine.

Anne artfully returned his comments with a sassy quip, "Oh, I get that all the time, Mr. Lewis."

At that, Betts had to fake a cough to keep from laughing and dig in her purse for her water bottle so she could turn her head away from the two of them. Mr. Lewis, sworn to secrecy, pledged his allegiance to Anne promising never to tell anyone that once upon a time in Hollywood, she was a movie double for the famous Lyla Fontaine in many a James Bond Movie.

Lyla concluded her deal with Herb Lewis, Village manager, "Thank you Mr. Lewis. The paparazzi have often made my life miserable. I'm so thankful for this little slice of paradise to protect me from the constant barrage of Lyla's fans."

Anne Knight played the roll convincingly and Betts told Ruth, "I could hardly keep from applauding and giving her a standing 'O'!"

Chapter 6

Johnson Kennedy's last dutiful act, before backing out of his father's driveway, onto Sunset Lane was to double check Smith's daily pill dispenser. He made sure that all slots were filled for two weeks, every morning, noon and evening and yet, he was hesitant leaving his father alone as he turned south past the Venus De Milo and giant aqua-marine seashell bidding him a friendly *Good-Bye and Please Drive Safely.*

Signing ownership papers for the Putt-Putt proved to be as smooth of a transaction as the two men had expected. All Smith had to do was wave cash under the owner's nose and the whole place was his in a matter of just a few days. Johnson smiled remembering it was only a few minutes after the for-sale sign came down that his father's cell phone rang.

"Hi there! Can I talk to the new owner?" quipped a perky voice.

"This is he," Smith said with a bit of hesitation.

"Well, hi there, boss! It's your manager-in-training checkin' in to see when you're wantin' me to report for duty!" Smith was silent, trying to decipher who was on the other end of the line, "Hey, don't ya remember me? It's Crystal, Crystal Bell! I'm on my break over here at the diner and saw ya out there in the parkin' lot."

"OH! Miss Bell, Miss Crystal Bell, I could never forget you!" blurted Smith.

"Well boss, the sign came down and you told me to call ya when it did. Do I still have that job you offered?"

"Miss Bell, if you can be here Saturday morning at 8:00 a.m. I'll start you at a dollar more than minimum wage and if all goes well, we'll do what we can to get you moved up to management. That will look good on a college application, young lady!" Smith was always delighted with enthusiastic youth.

"Holy cats! Boss! I'll be there. See you Saturday, eight o'clock sharp." Crystal did a little jig on the other end of the phone line. "If you need any help at all, anytime, I'm your girl just gimme a call. You got my number?"

"I've got it, Miss Bell, right here on my caller ID. I look forward to working with you," Smith smiled as he hung up the phone.

Smith and Johnson had walked through the eighteen-hole course noting the extensive improvements that needed to be made. It would be a few months before everything would be completed but, in their sketches, the Putt-Putt would be developed into a family-friendly course. In the meantime, Smith would practice putting and work hard on the therapy plan he and his Physical Therapist had laid out together. Crystal would be assigned some administrative duties and run errands to begin. Both Smith and Johnson knew she would become a great company asset when the hiring process began. Crystal had the scoop on everyone and would recommend reliable hires. A quality staff would provide an even more enjoyable experience at the newly remodeled Arcadia Putt-Putt.

Miss Crystal Bell would also be the sleeping pill Johnson would focus on during those late-night hours when he would lay in bed worrying about his father's health and well-being. He regretted that he didn't have the teen's phone number as yet, but he would retrieve it from Smith's caller ID when he had the chance. With Crystal's number added to his contacts list he would feel more settled about leaving his father alone in Arcadia. Johnson encouraged his father to get involved in some of the Village activities. "You might as well get to know a few people, Dad; chat it up with the neighbors. You're here on your own for a while." If Smith would make a few acquaintances in the Village, night or day, someone would be looking out for him.

Little did Johnson or Smith know that as the Highlander backed out of the driveway onto Sunset

Lane, one of those new neighbors was already interested in making that acquaintance.

Chapter 7

Betty watched Johnson make his way past Venus De Milo and the giant seashell sign from the chair on her front porch. It appeared as though the younger man left the older man with no noticeable means of transportation except a golf cart. Top of the line golf cart, but still, she questioned, *no car*? That was a mystery she intended to investigate. Normally, she wouldn't have been suspicious about a new neighbor and would have gone herself to offer assistance but now that Lyla Fontaine was a resident of the Arcadia Retirement Village, her guard was up and nerves on edge. She didn't trust anyone, especially an attractive single man suspiciously moving into a cottage across the street from the actress the same week that she had made Sunset Lane her residence. Life for Beatrice, assistant to the stars, had not been that coincidental. There was always an angle.

Having no car meant one of two things in Betty's skeptical mind: One, this fellow either lost his license due to health or drunk driving or, two, he was working as a dubious Hollywood insider and followed Lyla with plans to reveal her where-abouts, plastering details all over the media. Betty slipped into the house and peered through her bedroom window with binoculars. She surveyed the new neighbor from head to toe. He looked perfectly healthy to her; although, it was a bit difficult to get a good straight-on view from behind the blinds hanging in her bedroom window. But the longer she studied the man, the more convinced she was that the latter of the two options was the case. When he lifted a hospital cane from his golf cart Betty determined it was a prop, a Hollywood stunt to look sickly enough to be in need of Lyla's attention when he went knocking on her door. He stepped inside but quickly reappeared on his front porch without the cane and leaned against the rail looking up and down the street as if waiting for some incredulous film crew to locate him.

As he lingered on the front porch of the ocean blue cottage, Betty studied him carefully refocusing the binoculars on his facial features, he looked vaguely familiar. She realized she had seen this malefactor before and was sure she had seen him on TV, most likely some news show. Her thoughts led her to only one conclusion; he had to be a reporter assigned to find out the condition and where-abouts of Lyla Fontaine.

Betty felt the inner Beatrice, protector and procurer of privacy for Lyla Fontaine, rise to the surface. The more she thought about it, the more obvious it became; his plan would be to get close to Lyla or Anne or whatever her friend would call herself, become friendly asking for innocent rides to the doctor's office (everyone at the Village went to the doctor) followed up by a visit to the pharmacy of course, followed by a stop at the Arcadia Diner for a chat over coffee, followed by the season finale of Access Hollywood for the big reveal! (Although Betty never acted, she always enjoyed the drama.)

Betty, who had also assisted other stars from the James Bond film series, decided to use the skills she learned from Mr. Bond and launch an all-out Hollywood style, secret investigation on this new neighbor. And, for now, until she could pinpoint this fellow, she decided to keep this knowledge from Lyla, now Anne, saving her from anxiety and shielding her tenuous heart. She would rely on unwitting Village residents to do the investigating and would start at the source of all Village information: Dolores Barnes.

Dolores Barnes, the Village office secretary, was behind her desk when Betty parked in one of the three parking spots at the Arcadia Retirement Village office. The sign above the door on the building simply read, "Village Office" so there was no question that village information could be acquired inside. Betty arrived at

12:03 p.m. knowing that Herb would have gone home to have lunch and take Bootsie the Pomeranian for her afternoon walk two streets over. He would be back in his assigned office chair by 12:55 p.m. giving Betty just enough time to pique Dolores's curiosity about the single, handsome renter in the ocean blue cottage on Sunset Lane. If she could get Dolores's curiosity stirred, wondering about the availability of this possibly eligible fellow, she might be able to retrieve some background information about her new neighbor. She could suggest to the widow Dolores that he was lonely and seeking consolation in the Village, influencing her to dip into his file and reveal some background information that Betty could use on him before he divulged Lyla to the world.

Betty started talking before she had even stepped through the doorway, "Dolores, you really need to give me the number to the salon where you have your hair done, dear. You look ten years younger! If you keep going, you're going to have to show your driver's license at the Village gate to prove you're old enough to live here!"

Both ladies laughed and Dolores blushed slightly as she smoothed her bangs over to one side and tucked them behind her ear. She wasn't a vain woman, but a compliment from a woman like Betty meant something. No one knew much about Betty's past at Arcadia

Retirement Village but she was different than most of the others who came from Ohio or Michigan or Ontario, Canada. She was clearly not your typical Midwest grandmother-type. She never wore black tennis shoes with footie socks or sweatshirts adorned with fake collars and seasonal embellishments. Although she tried, Dolores couldn't even conjure up a picture in her mind of Betty riding a giant three-wheeler with an orange traffic flag waving off the back like many of the other Villagers were prone to do. When Betty left her cottage, she always had a bit of rouge brushed into the hollow of her cheeks, a touch of eye shadow, plucked brows and perfectly shaded lip color. But even beyond her physical appearance there was something worldly and wise that accompanied Betty; an elegance and poise to her that came from somewhere far beyond the stucco wall that surrounded the Village.

Betty leaned over the desk and questioned Dolores a bit longer about the salon then segued into questions about the new neighbor on Sunset Lane. "So, if my neighbor would like to freshen up his look, could he go to your salon, or is it strictly women only?"

"Which neighbor is looking for a new look, Betty?" Dolores raised an eyebrow and Betty was afraid she should have been a bit smoother on that transition.

"You know that handsome new gentleman that moved onto Sunset Lane, Mr..., Oh, Mr.... Please forgive me, Dolores, I'm just having a bit of trouble with my short-term memory today." Short-term memory loss was a great excuse that could be used for any occasion in the Village. "Mr. ..."

"Oh, do you mean Mr. Smith? Leonard Smith? Yes, of course. He's a handsome one, and single, too. I don't think he needs a new look at all Betty!" Betty made a mental note *Leonard Smith*. That name did not ring a bell, but she wasn't surprised. A good reporter would remain incognito during the investigation. She would have to dig a bit deeper.

"So, what do you know about handsome Mr. Smith, Dolores?" She followed that question with a deliberate wink. Her crafty plan to interest Dolores in the reporter was beginning to come to fruition. She noted the winsome smile appearing on the widow Dolores Barnes's bright red lips.

Unfortunately, Dolores had not read Betty's wink as a signal for herself to pursue Mr. Smith, "Why, Betty, in the four years you've been living here I have never known you to show an interest in any man in the Village. This fellow is a handsome one though. Maybe he's available!"

Betty just about fell backwards off her Prada flip-flops. She sputtered a bit trying to turn the attention of Mr. Smith to Dolores and away from her. She was not the least bit interested in men at her age, especially a no good, Hollywood insider! But before she could get her footing in the conversation Dolores continued, "Let's just find out a little bit about this mysterious hunk that has turned your head!"

Betty shut her mouth. If pretending to be interested in Mr. Smith would get those files opened, she would take the blow one more time for Lyla Fontaine. She forced a smile, "Oh, yes, let's do just that. You're a sly detective, you are!"

Dolores looked at the clock, "We've only got a few minutes before Herb gets back from lunch. He'll be winding up his walk with Bootsie soon. She pushed her desk chair with both feet and rolled backwards on all four wheels making a ninety degree turn in the seat and landing at a complete stop at the file drawer. It was quite an impressive move for someone of Village age. Dolores fingered through the file folders until she found Smith, Leonard. "Oh my!" she uttered with a blink.

"What is it?" Betty questioned as her heart pumped a little more quickly. This would be it; she could get this fellow before he got to Lyla. "Dolores, what's going on? Is he a spy, a convict, a millionaire?" Her quick thinking added millionaire to the list knowing that millionaires didn't live in places like Arcadia Retirement Village unless they were Lyla Fontaine in hiding as Anne Knight.

Dolores looked up, "Well, maybe any one of those things, Betty." She held up a file tucked into a sealed manila envelope with "SMITH, Leonard" printed neatly in Herb's handwriting in the upper right corner. The ladies heard a golf cart whir into the parking lot. Herb pulled into the spot marked with a *Village Manager* parking sign. Dolores flashed an apologetic smile and slid the file back into the drawer, closed it and whirled her chair back across the office in an impressive backwards motion just as the office door opened.

"Well, Hello ladies." Herb smiled and stood a bit straighter when he realized one of the ladies was Betty Brown. "And what can I do for you today, Ms. Brown?"

Betty began to say something polite that would hold Herb at bay for now but Dolores cut her off, "Hey, Herb," she began casually, "Betty is thinking of throwing a little party for new residents since she's the lucky recipient of new neighbors this month on Sunset Lane." Betty was shocked, jaw-droppingly shocked at Dolores's ability to lie so convincingly. "Can we get some info on that Mr.... Oh, what's his name, Herb, that new resident? Mr., hmmm, Smith? Is it Smith?"

Betty stammered an agreement and thought about Dolores on the big screen. She was a natural, very convincing. Dolores had missed her calling. Herb's back was to the ladies by this time and Dolores nodded a wink at Betty.

Herb kept his back turned and fumbled through some papers on his desk. He was not nearly as convincing in his ability to lie as Dolores. "Umm, yes, Smith, yes. Well, I'm not sure, umm, he's just a man that moved here from up north somewhere." Herb winced as he said those words remembering that everyone living in Arcadia was from up north somewhere. "He's just some guy, person, nothing special about him...he's just retired, and he liked the atmosphere here. He might like to golf or something."

As Herb rambled on, saying nothing at all, with his back still to them, Betty and Dolores exchanged questioning glances. Betty put her thumb to her ear and pinky finger to her lips as if holding a phone and mouthed the words *I'll call you* to Dolores.

"Don't you worry about it, Mr. Lewis, we won't bother Mr. What's-his-name, I was just trying to be a good neighbor and welcome him to the Village along with my friend Anne. I saw a moving van down the next block a few weeks ago as well. I just thought I'd get a few of the new folks connected to our activities." She knew that would smolder in Herb for a while. He made it a point to always invite the newbies to the Club House to get involved in canasta group, dog walking club, reading and discussion groups, or whatever was the going activity that month. Herb was a smart manager and knew it was good business for the Village to have the residents feel connected almost immediately. Betty didn't give him time to return an answer, though. With those words spoken she turned to Dolores as she stepped outside, "Don't forget, I need the number to your salon, dear," and shut the office door behind her.

It wasn't long before Betty's phone rang and the caller ID voice announced, "Call from Arcadia Village Office, call from Arcadia Village Office."

Betty answered, "Hello?"

"Betty, this is Dolores in the Village office. It worked! You are going to get your info on that man of yours." Betty cringed, glad that Dolores couldn't see her face. "Herb is going to be stopping by your place while on his walk with Bootsie later this evening. He's planning to ask if you'll be the hostess at a new neighbors get-together in the Club House. I knew you'd be excited so I just couldn't wait! I had to tell you myself."

"A get-together in the Club House?" Betty tried to respond with a smile even though she was speaking into her cell phone. She would at least sound happy, but this is the last thing she wanted. She was trying to keep Lyla's identity under wraps and inviting the whole of Arcadia Retirement Village to be up-close and personal with her was not part of that plan. If one fan would make one phone call to one news agency, it would be all over. And, most likely, this Mr. What's-his-name Smith would be the one to do it!

Chapter 8

Smith wound his way through the Village, first past the Venus De Milo now draped in a red Valentine scarf dotted with pink hearts then the giant aqua-marine seashell bidding him to drive safely and come again. Rather than crossing Highway 70 at the traffic light, the path he travelled paralleled the main road. His new Club Car golf cart was top of the line and as comfortable as any convertible he had driven. It was decked out with accessories such as an under the dash fan, black diamond plate rocker panels, an aviator carbon fiber steering wheel with a large rearview mirror as well as side mirrors to clearly see traffic coming up behind him. Smith topped off the sleek look of his new ride with aluminum wheels and a set of Michelin tires that rode like a dream. His only regret was giving into his son's request that he drive electric and not gas until his physical therapy was completed. Johnson was worried he might be tempted to use more horsepower than needed before he was fully recovered.

The ride to the Putt-Putt was less than fifteen minutes from driveway to door. Smith made his way past the Piggly Wiggly and skirted the edge of the Arcadia Plaza. Arcadia Retirement Village was the ideal place for him during the weeks of therapy. The local bank, Tony's Fried chicken, Arcadia Pharmacy and the Dollar Spot were all nestled in the Piggly Wiggly plaza. These were not the stores at which Smith had been accustomed to shopping, but they certainly had everything he needed. On the far side of the parking lot was Mary Jean Drive. If he turned right, it was only a block to Christ the King Community Church where he could join parishioners for Sunday morning worship service. However, crossing Mary Jean Drive at the traffic light led him directly to the Putt-Putt office and parking lot.

As Smith waited at the corner for the light to change, he glanced up at oncoming traffic. Slowing to a stop as the light changed from yellow to red was the silver Porsche he had seen delivered on Sunset Lane in the Village. But more importantly, behind the steering wheel, her head turned in his direction, sat the familiar woman who had waved at him.

Smith crossed Mary Jean Drive and pulled the Club Car next to the Putt-Putt office just as the Porsche's blinker popped on and turned in his direction. He climbed out of the Club Car and stood up leaving his cane on the passenger's seat. The Porsche maneuvered in next to him and the driver's tinted window slowly dropped revealing an extraordinarily stunning woman about Smith's age. Her silver white hair was pulled back in a bright blue scarf that matched bold blue sunglasses. The driver flashed an electrifying smile with a small space between her front teeth that seemed tremendously familiar to Smith.

Smith's mind raced to think of something intelligent to say as he pleaded with his brain to get beyond the effects of the stroke. He opened his mouth to offer a pleasant 'Hello," but as he did the Putt-Putt office door swung open and out bounded Crystal Bell, "Hey! You two know each other?" She barely touched the steps as she landed between the Porsche and the Club Car, "I was just thinkin' the other day that I oughta get y'all together and make a grand ole introduction but maybe you did that yerselves? Did ya?"

Smith smiled at the teen's exuberance. "Crystal Bell, I have not had the pleasure of meeting this young lady yet, would you like to make the introductions?" he said as cavalierly as possible.

"But only if you think this gentleman is fitting to be introduced," Lyla proffered as she lifted her sunglasses revealing a twinkle in her eyes. With that she winked, a mischievous little side wink and Smith remembered where he had seen her! He knew exactly who was sitting in the driver's seat of a silver Porsche in the parking lot of his Putt-Putt Golf Course but, before his thought could be formed into words Crystal waved her arms in grand fashion and the introductions tumbled out like someone had just pulled the plug on a drain.

"Ms. Anne Knight let me introduce you to my boss..." Crystal continued the introduction with a story about meeting them both at the diner before they moved into the Village, but confusion muted the conversation for Smith.

Anne? Anne who? This woman is not Anne, she's Lyla. This is Lyla Fontaine! Smith knew who this was, he had seen her in the movies and admittedly had a bit of a crush on her before he met Claire. They had even attended the same Hollywood pool party in the early days of his career, before anyone really knew who he was except for the good folks from Kellogg's Cereal who had signed the promising golf star as a sponsor. He clearly remembered watching her glide person-to-person from across the pool. She approached the Hollywood royalty of the day with ease while on the arm of James Bond, of course. For a moment that day, she had noticed his interest and while James Bond chatted with partiers at his table, she smiled at Smith from across the pool, and then winked. He wanted to introduce himself but his confidence off the golf course waned, especially in Hollywood, so he left the party having only responded to her acknowledgement of him with a nod. The starlet had been far, far out of his league.

He jerked back to reality as she said, "Hello Leonard, nice to meet you."

For a split-second in his confusion, Smith wondered, *who's Leonard*? As he was grappling in his mind for a rational thought process he smiled and nodded in bewilderment.

"Golly boss, you okay? You look like you lost yer dog or somethin'."

"Sorry," Smith managed, "I thought you were someone else. It's nice to meet you..." he stuttered trying to remember the name Crystal said, "very nice to meet you, miss...ma'am, um..."

"Anne," Lyla graciously offered her name again even though she knew Smith was aware and confused by her Hollywood identity, "Anne Knight." Lyla smiled and continued the charade in front of Crystal Bell, "And it has been my pleasure to meet you as well," she paused ever so briefly, "Mr. Smith." She knew this man's name was not Leonard Smith. She would never have parked her Porsche in a Putt-Putt parking lot in Arcadia, Florida to speak with a *Leonard Smith*. "I hope we have the opportunity to talk and maybe even to trade stories, soon." The window was raised as Smith replayed the short conversation in his head. Crystal took over the moment blurting out a list of "to do's" and phone call messages as Smith watched the Porsche make its way back to Highway 70, past the giant seashell and Venus De Milo as it turned toward Sunset Lane.

Chapter 9

There was a knock on the screen door followed by "Anybody home? Are you here Ms. Brown?"

Betty had left the front door open to catch the cool February breeze. She leaned her head around the kitchen corner to see Herb and Bootsie peering in from her front steps. Herb was wearing his Arcadia Village Manager name tag, so she knew he had arrived carrying out official Village business.

"Hello, Herb. Good to see you too, Bootsie." She opened the front door and Herb backed down off the porch. "Would you like to come in?"

"No, no, not with Boots, here. I just wanted to take you up on your offer, Ms. Brown. The offer of entertaining the newcomers." Herb averted his eyes and gazed off to the side as if he were having a marvelous brainstorm at that precise moment. He tried hard to appear as if heaven itself was downloading directives during a short contemplative pause. He turned back to Betty and continued his official business. "Ms. Brown, I have the most wonderful idea. I would love to have you host a New Neighbors gathering at the Club House next week. The Village will provide the desserts, of course, and coffee, then we'll give the new-comers the opportunity to introduce themselves, and ..."

"Herb," Betty interrupted the volcanic flow of ideas that he was spewing. She was from Hollywood, she knew what he was trying to accomplish with his over-dramatized pause, "Herb," she repeated to be sure she had stopped the flow, at least momentarily, "I was just going to have my two new neighbors come for pie and coffee. You know, Anne, my dear friend and the new fellow down the street, Mr. Smith...I think that's his name." She echoed Herb's pause appearing as if she was now searching for some heavenly sign concerning this man's name. "I was just trying to get his information to invite just the two of them..."

"Ms. Brown, please, let's consider the broader picture. It is far bigger than *just* those two." Herb had been concerned about keeping the secrets bestowed on him by Anne, the Lyla Fontaine double and Leonard Smith, the commercial king. He had heard the gossip across the pool patio and around the Club House card tables. The men wove stories about the stunning new woman in the pink cottage on Sunset Lane and the women told their own tales about the plastic surgery, nips, and tucks that had to have been taken over the years. Unfortunately, the ladies' stories didn't stop there, either. They continued their folklore as they discussed the familiar face of the man in the classy and obviously expensive new Club Car that he drove to the old Putt-Putt.

Alma Jean told Herb over the counter in the Village Office that the extravagant golf cart could be seen at the Putt-Putt all day, every day. She confessed to the office staff that she had begun parking in the southwest corner of the Piggly Wiggly parking lot to get an inconspicuous look at the miniature golf course as she hoisted her fresh vegetables and groceries into her own golf cart every few days. "He's there all the time, Herb, and making quite a project of it. What's he up to and where did he come from?" She demanded a response, "You must know something, Herbert. What's the big secret?"

Herb had lost a bit of sleep worrying about the amount of attention being drawn to the two newcomers. His 2:43 a.m. brainstorm was what finally gave him peace; he would hide them in plain sight. He believed that to be the only logical answer for curbing the Village buzz.

He explained all of this to Betty hoping to appeal to her protective influence over her friend Anne Knight, "If all the new Village residents were introduced at the same time, Ms. Knight would not appear so reclusive and conspicuous. She is a striking woman, and many have not just noticed, Ms. Brown, but have been asking a lot of questions. I understand that she is here to enjoy a peaceful retirement but her mysterious air has caused quite a lot of noise throughout our quiet, serene community. If others could speak with her, befriend her, why, she may just be considered one of us, and left in peace. Oh, Ms. Brown, you just don't know the pressure I'm under from the likes of Blanche Thompson and some of the ladies in her, shall I say, her following."

He couldn't tell Betty that Leonard desired the same innocuous lifestyle. He had to rely on his persuasive skills and appeal to her protective instincts. He hoped using Blanche's name would convince Betty this party would be in the best interest for her friend. "Ms. Brown, you're the one hostess who could pull this off."

Betty felt her stomach tighten and her heart sink. She hated the idea that Herb might be right, especially about Blanche Thompson, and reluctantly conceded to his appeals. If Lyla Fontaine could be introduced face-to-face to the folks of Arcadia Village as Anne Knight, in the Club House under red Valentine hearts hanging from pink crepe paper streamers, her secret might remain secret. Plus, it may send Mr. Mystery Man down the street packing. Betty was sure he would respond to the invitation to meet Anne Knight. Like all the others, he would jump at the chance to get to know the beauty in the pink cottage on Sunset Lane.

Dolores sent out the email notice to all of Arcadia Retirement Villagers and posted the familiar printed flyers that hung on all the Village bulletin boards:

"MEET YOUR NEW NEIGHBORS"
JOIN US AT THE CLUB HOUSE FOR PIE & COFFEE
(DECAF PROVIDED)
WEDNESDAY AT 7:00P.M.

Meetyournewneighborpartieswereheldthroughout the year at Arcadia Village and hosted by one of the Village staff so there was nothing conspicuous about the event except for the new neighbors themselves. The office staff ordered extra Marie Callender's pies and brewed sixty cups of decaf coffee along with a couple of extra pots of regular, knowing that curiosity would bring a larger crowd than usual. There were five new residents to the Village being welcomed at this get-together. Anne Knight and Leonard Smith were joined by a lovely couple, Susan and David Willoughby, who moved from England, and Ellwood McCoy, a West Virginia native.

The Club House was packed by 6:45. Golf carts overflowed the adjoining lot and were parked up and down the curb. Men hurried to grab a piece of pie before the table was emptied of the favorites. The new residents would be brought to the small stage at the front of the meeting room and invited to sit in metal folding chairs with brightly colored cushions.

Betty had lectured Lyla all afternoon concerning the introductory speech she would be invited to give. "Keep it short! Do you hear me, Anne, S-H-O-R-T, short! You are not accepting an Oscar, you are Anne Knight and you have NO life to expound on, you are just giving your name and thanking everyone for being kind neighbors."

Lyla laughed and smiled, "Oh, Betty, dear, it will be my finest performance."

"NO!" Betty sighed, "Don't make this a dramatic performance, just keep it short and sweet, ANNE! SHORT and SWEET! For once in your life, don't draw attention to yourself." Lyla knew Betty truly meant business when she concluded, "If I have to, I'll call Betts, Lyla. I WILL call Betts! Let's just play this cool and casual, cool and casual. Like Herb said, 'You may just become one of us', but you have to act the part of a Villager to be welcomed as one. No performance, nothing Lyla, all ANNE tonight. Please remember this is about my sanity as much as yours. You were only to come here under wraps! No show, no cameras, no LYLA!"

Lyla merely smiled. Betty was sure she could visibly see the wheels turning in her mind. She knew her friend was mulling over a plan and no matter how she threatened or pleaded, Lyla would do what she wanted.

With a deep sigh Betty concluded her instruction, "I'll pick you up at 6:30, I have to arrive early as the hostess, and remember, I'm stuck being the hostess because of you! Now, cool and casual!"

At 6:30 Lyla slid into the golf cart next to Betty. She wore a daffodil yellow chiffon top with a scoop neck over white and yellow striped capris. Silver hair tumbled over her daisy print scarf tied neatly around her neck, a diamond necklace hung at her neckline. The Louis Vuitton sling backs matched the bag she threw over her shoulder. She pulled her sunglasses down from the top of her head releasing her soft curls and smiled at Betty, "How do I look? Cool and casual?"

"UGH! Anne, you are supposed to be Anne. How are we going to hide you in yellow and Louis Vuitton, Lyla? That outfit screams, 'Look at me, I'm loaded with money, sex-appeal and fame!' No, that is not Village cool or Village casual. You are supposed to be in Village attire. Now go put on blue jeans and a CASUAL top! Right now! Blend, Anne Knight, blend!"

Lyla huffed her way back to the pink cottage and returned in blue jean capris with a ruffled hem and a fitted denim button-down with embroidered pocket. She refused to give up Louis Vuitton's company, however, and she still wore the sparkling diamond teardrop around her neck. As she defiantly slid back into the cart Betty let out a quiet groan.

"What?" Lyla demanded.

"This will never work, ANNE, you can't hide Hollywood!"

Lyla smiled and winked sideways at Betty, "Just watch me, dear, it'll all be fine!"

They arrived as the building was filling up. Betty immediately rolled into hostess mode, "Hello, Dolores. Great to see you here tonight, Stanly. Oh, Gladdy, I love that top. You look divine. Now all of you help yourself to coffee and pie. Well, it looks like you've been helping yourself already Max!" Betty had hosted many a Hollywood gala, but in the back of her mind she was worried that this party might be her most trying.

Lyla stepped through the door and immediately went into character. As Anne she became a bit demure but couldn't help flashing a coy smile with lips kept shut, at just the right moments. Residents milled about the room taking their places with friends.

Blanche Thompson arrived early enough to claim one of the armchairs in the corner and gave a play-by-play of Anne's every move. "Did you see her shift her weight from one foot to the other? Must have had that hip replaced a few years ago, although it could have been a knee. Did you get a look at the costume jewelry? Hmmm, I wonder who she's trying to impress. She is quite thin, must either be a drinker or have one of those eating disorders like June's granddaughter who was sent to rehab. She's drinking decaf, no, no wait, regular, and with Splenda and she is not having pie. There's something not quite right about not having a piece of Marie Callender's at your own party..."

Anne noticed the group gathered around Blanche like a posse. They held to her every word, so she mingled her way over to them. "Hello ladies, how are all of you this evening?'

Watching from across the room, just like he had done at the Hollywood pool all those years earlier, Smith finally conjured up the confidence he had lacked and decided it was time to approach Lyla Fontaine.

As the ladies were humming and hawing trying to cover their rancorous conversation before Lyla's 'hello', Smith ended his conversation with a group of balding men who had cornered him with questions about the Club Car he drove. He sidled up to the ladies and he leaned into the group with one shoulder looking into each guilt-ridden face. He was an attractive man who seldom used his sex appeal for anything other than selling razors and golf shoes on television but he took full advantage of his good looks as he smiled at the group of gossips and took Anne by the arm. "Excuse me ladies, I had the pleasure of starting a conversation with this lovely lady the other day but never had the opportunity to finish it. May I steal her away?"

As he turned Anne away Blanche raised an eyebrow in disapproval, "I think we can guess where that is leading." The posse agreed.

"Oh, you ruined it! I had them on the run, Mr. Smith." Lyla smiled that sideways smile at him and winked.

"Okay, okay," he smirked, "Miss Anne, or whatever you want to call yourself these days, we need to talk. I want to know your story..." Then he dropped his voice to a low whisper and concluded his sentence, "Lyla."

"Lyla?" She whispered back, "Why, what do mean? Did you hear that on the golf course? Oh, and I don't mean Putt-Putt golf course, Mr. Kennedy."

At that moment Herb's voice came over the loudspeaker, "Thank you everyone for coming tonight, what a great turn out! And a special thank you to Ms. Brown for organizing such a lovely event. The Valentine streamers and hearts have certainly put us in a festive mood this evening. I have to add that Bootsie and I have been enjoying all the Valentine décor throughout our neighborhood. And whoever is responsible for adding the Valentine touches to our Venus De Milo, well, she certainly welcomes newcomers, doesn't she?" The room chuckled and Betty noticed Dolores blushing and giving a bashful wave. "Speaking of welcoming newcomers, we'd love to have our new residents and neighbors come up to the podium and introduce themselves at this time."

The five filed to the stage and sat in the assigned row of folding chairs. The Willoughbys spoke first. "Ello, all. We're not from around here, if you couldn't tell." The room chuckled as David continued in his heavy British accent. "We arrived in the States 'bout six weeks ago from the North of London. Settled here in the Village to be quite near our children and grandchildren in Punta Gorda. They're a couple o' rascals, those li'le ones. But we're pleased to be out here, away from the tourist hubbub. We 'ad enough o' that in jolly ole England, you know, with the Queen livin' just up the road." He smiled and more chuckles rose from the crowd. "We missed our children terribly and spent all our holiday here in Florida with them, what a shame to be so far away. Then Mum here," he pointed to Susan who smiled and waved, "came up with the brilliant idea to make the move and come out for good, and 'Bob's your uncle' here we are! You Americans look like a lot o' good ole blokes. We're hopin' to find a couple o' good mates here, hope that'll be some of you," David concluded.

Esther Wilson leaned close to her husband and whispered, "They're looking for mates? I thought they were married. What will their children think?"

Everyone else nodded in approval of the Willoughbys, although they weren't sure about "Uncle Bob," whoever that was, but everyone was glad to hear they could now spend more than just a holiday with family.

Leonard Smith rose, left his cane next to his chair and moved to the microphone. He removed his golf hat to reveal a head of salt and pepper hair and handsome brown eyes. Esther leaned back to her husband and whispered again, "I'll bet if Mrs. Willoughby is looking for a mate, she hopes it's him!"

"Hello," he began.

Betty scrutinized his every move. He was poised and polished as he used the microphone. *But of course,* she thought. *He's a reporter!*

"I'm Leonard Smith. I'm here in the Village on assignment."

What? Betty couldn't believe her ears. Was he inadvertently admitting that he was on an assignment from some news program? Obviously, he was already making his move to reveal Lyla! Betty pulled her golf cart key out of her pocket. She kicked off her Prada flip flops, ready to grab Lyla and make a break for it before the cameras showed up.

Blanche leaned into her cohorts and nodded in Betty's direction, "I knew those fancy shoes had to be painful on those bunions."

"The company I work for designs golf courses," Smith continued, "and I'm here for a few months assigned to get that Putt-Putt up and running. Let me ask, how many of you had a first date at a Putt-Putt golf course?" About half the room smiled, sighed and raised a hand. "It's a tradition that most of us have lived out in our, well should I say, our earlier years. Did you know that teenagers continue to have first dates at Putt-Putt golf courses still today? We'd like to see kids in this area have that same experience. However, in a few months, when the place is finished, I'll be on my way. But it's great to be here for now."

Whispers of sentimental approval could be heard all over the room.

"Hmmm, good cover," Betty whispered to Dolores who was standing next to her in the kitchen doorway.

"What?" Dolores looked puzzled at Betty and Betty suddenly realized whose ear she was whispering into. "What do you mean by that?"

"I think he's...running from the law...or something like that," Betty whispered back. She couldn't tell Dolores that he was a reporter and she couldn't think of anything else to say at the moment. She hoped Dolores would just drop the whole thought.

"What?" Dolores drew back, "He's what?"

Out of desperation, Betty responded to her puzzled friend with a giggled whisper, "Ha! Got ya!" She hoped that was enough for Dolores to forget the whole conversation.

At that moment, Herb motioned for Lyla to come to the microphone.

Lyla blew into the microphone and thumped it with her finger. A high pierced squeal set off hearing aids around the room, "Hello, can you all hear me?" The crowded room nodded, and many held a finger to their ears. "Oh, good. My name is Anne Knight and I want all of you Villagers to know just how beautiful you are."

"Is she talking to me?" ninety-two-year-old, Howard Nivens asked the fellow next him. He sat up as straight as he could and cocked his ear in her direction.

"I'm so glad to have found the Arcadia Retirement Village. It's my utopia, a wonderland filled with such marvelous neighbors. Let me confess to you," Lyla lowered her voice before she continued, "I've lived... well, such a difficult life for so long I've forgotten what a sweet pleasure it is to stroll down a quiet street and wave hello to a kindred spirit." She lifted her hand and waved it as her voice floated through the room and seemed to trail off mournfully. Every eye was on her not knowing they were witnessing one of the greats. Howard Nivens, mistaking her gesture, waved back.

Betty dropped her head and began to pray, *Oh Lord, make her stop!* Lyla was piecing together memorized lines from a myriad of movies she had filmed over the years.

Betty shook her head as her eyes met Lyla's but knew there was no stopping her now; Lyla Fontaine was on a roll.

"It is a gift to have a friend, a confidant, to have someone willing to rescue me from a life of turmoil and love me as no other friend has," she smiled and nodded directly at Betty.

Once again, Blanche raised an eyebrow at the ladies around her. Esther leaned again to whisper in her husband's ear, "So, are they mates?"

"Oh, my friends, my dear, new friends, what a delight it is to have you all as my neighbors, let us celebrate our lives together in this faaabulous garden paradise known as Arcadia Village." Lyla lifted her arms, palms to the sky and opened them in a grand gesture to include the entire room. She wiped a tear from her eye as she concluded, "Thank you all for welcoming me so warmly into your lives."

Betty began to understand, Lyla was masterfully isolating herself from all the other Villagers. Blanche would begin the grapevine chatter before they left the building and Anne Knight would be labeled "a little too eccentric" for the Village.

Smith leaned forward in his folding chair and cocked his head to get a better view of Lyla's face. He was baffled and his expression didn't hide his bewilderment. His eyes followed her back to her seat and met hers and she smiled. The shared look did not escape Betty.

Blanche began whispering to the woman next to her and Esther leaned into her husband's ear then pulled back again. She couldn't think of a thing to say.

After a moment of awkward silence, Herb motioned to Ellwood and he stepped up to the microphone. "Uh, yeah, I don't, uh, like to talk much. I'm Ellwood McCoy, I uh, came down from West Virginia. I ain't got nothin' up there anymore. The wife passed and the kids moved out. I uh, I guess that's it."

Beads of perspiration began forming on Herb's brow, "Well, a big round of applause for our new neighbors. You are quite an interesting group. Thank you all for sharing a bit of yourselves with us. Um, yes. Please, finish up the pie all." Herb stepped back and wiped his forehead with his hanky.

Chapter 10

The crowd milled around the Club House a while longer exchanging their own stories about moving to Arcadia Retirement Village. Most couples gravitated to the seemingly ordinary Willoughbys. Aside from their English argot and British accents they seemed to be what mid-westerners call standard stock; the kind of people Arcadia Villagers appreciated being their "mates".

A few of the more serious golfers had questions for Leonard Smith and noted that he looked a bit like the famous golfer, Smith Kennedy, but they all knew Smith Kennedy would never take up residence in a place like Arcadia Retirement Village. By-in-large it was the single ladies that gathered around him. A sudden surge of interest in improving one's Putt-Putt golf score became the topic of conversation in his company and a few of the bold even asked for private lessons, Dolores included. After the party she confessed to Blanche that she was inquiring for Betty and requested her conversation with Leonard Smith be kept hush-hush. Although Blanche nodded in agreement, Dolores worried.

Foregoing the decaf, Ellwood poured himself a full cup of high-octane coffee and moved quietly alone to a corner. He silently slipped out through the Club House side door evading any conversation in which he might have to engage.

A few kinder souls nodded hello to Lyla, but kept their distance and their voices low, in a polite sort of way. Howard Nivens, enamored by the idea that the lovely woman at the microphone had paid attention to him, was the only resident to approach Lyla. Leaning on his walker he asked her for her name again and was considering the idea of inviting the beautiful lady to lunch.

With her hands full of paper plates and plastic forks she had collected from around the room, Betty pushed between the two with an "Excuse me," to Howard while nodding her head toward the Club House kitchen in a motion for Lyla to follow.

Lyla thanked Howard for coming over to say hello then excused herself to help with kitchen duties (although she had hoped she really wouldn't have to put her hands in dishwater or carry garbage bags to the dumpster).

"Masterfully played, Anne," Betty whispered, "Arcadia Retirement Villagers are all in agreement; you're a bit bizarre to be a Villager! You'll be kept anonymous, that's for sure."

As hostess for the evening, Betty was assigned to oversee the clean-up committee. She shooed Lyla Fontaine out the back-exit door while she washed dishes and straightened tables. Lyla found herself alone on Sunset Lane, enjoying the cool evening breeze blowing against her blushed cheeks as she walked under the stars that began to form a canopy above one-by-one.

Tidy houses lined the street and neatly trimmed palms rustled in the soft evening breeze. A bold pink and orange sunset dropped beyond the last cottage and faded into a deep purple sky. The scene reminded her of an old movie set, the sets that were once painted and blurred a bit in the filming to soften the stark colors adding an element of reality.

For Lyla, Arcadia Retirement Village had softened the reality of her heart attack and blurred the memory of the pain and fear that had held her in its grip. Staying in the Village had been comforting but when she tried thinking of the Village as home, her heart wouldn't accept it. As the pink and orange darkened into night, she tried saying the words out loud, "This is home," but to no avail.

Her home was a tastefully decorated mansion tucked away in Beverly Hills, where Betts was raised, and artists and actors came to have tea in the afternoon and cocktails in the evening. It was an extravagance for a girl from Swartz Creek, Michigan, but she alone labored hard and proudly fulfilled the demands of the substantial mortgage. With great artistic care she chose each piece of furniture and artwork so her home flowed with elegance from room-to-room, floor-to-floor. But Lyla's lifestyle, as that of any star that burned to the magnitude of Lyla Fontaine, hadn't allowed for the luxury of time to relax and enjoy all that she had accomplished. She was more often away filming on site in some distant city rather than delighting in the peaceful life she had managed to build for Betts and Maybelle Studer in the middle of the noise of Hollywood.

Arcadia Retirement Village was a far cry from her home in Beverly Hills. The quiet tranquility proved healing, and Lyla was regaining her strength without worry of schedules and photographers to manage. Acadia sheltered her from the barrage of questions from the press and from behind a desk in Los Angeles, Judy, her personal assistant, protected her from the onslaught of fan mail and constant requests for appearances. Arcadia was restoring her health and even her soul, but it wasn't home.

Lyla climbed the three steps to her front porch. She positioned herself in one of the padded chairs and leaned her back against a pillow brandishing a pink flamingo head. A brief twinge of loneliness tightened her shoulders and a feeling of homesickness washed over her as she looked at the stars dotting the night sky. Sitting alone with only the pink flamingo head to give her comfort and the darkened, purple sky overhead, she thought about the stars. *One day all of the stars in Hollywood will burn out just like all these stars that twinkle so brightly tonight.* It was with that thought, reality struck her: *and that includes me. One day I'm going to burn out,* she thought, and a tear rolled down her cheek. It was there on the front porch of the pink cottage with the flamingo head as her witness that Lyla prayed a new prayer. She simply said, "Help me, God. I don't want to fizzle like stardust, I want to blaze like a supernova." Lyla surprised herself, her prayer was uniquely her own, not a line from a script.

Golf carts rolled past, and a few voices shouted, "Welcome to the Village." Lyla smiled at them all and gave a neighborly wave. She wasn't sorry for her ridiculous introduction earlier in the evening, it would provide a distance between the other Villagers and herself and for that she breathed a thank you to heaven. She remembered Betty's plea to her to keep their fame a secret. Lyla Fontaine loved Betty Brown as much as Betty loved her. It would devastate Lyla if she were to upset the unpretentious lifestyle Betty was relishing in the Village. She looked over at her friend's bright yellow cottage across Sunset Lane with battery-operated candles gleaming in the living room window and thanked God for their friendship as she stepped inside the pink cottage and closed the door behind her.

Lyla locked the door because Betts had told her to, though she wasn't sure it was necessary. She had noticed Mr. McCoy sitting in the dark on his front porch as she passed by that evening, but the lonely man was hardly a threat. No one in the Village seemed to be a danger. She smiled to herself thinking that after her introduction she may be perceived as more dangerous than any of them. Her performance that evening had been short, but impressive and her muse, a character she played in one of the Bond movies; a poor young thing whose mind was being manipulated until 007 swept in by means of a rocket propelled jet pack and rescued her from the torment.

Lyla poured herself a glass of lemonade she had retrieved from the refrigerator, gathered her latest read and headed for the bedroom when there was a quiet knock on the front door. "Coming Betty," she called and opened the door prepared to discuss the reactions of the Villagers to the evening's events and talk about the prospects of discussing London with the Willoughbys.

She flipped the switch for the porch light and there in her doorway stood Smith Kennedy. She looked beyond him for the Club Car. She didn't want Betty to see it parked in her drive, next to the silver Porsche. Seeing it was in his own carport across the street she smiled, "What a surprise!"

"Good evening, Ms. Anne, Ms. Fontaine. Which is it now?" Smith hadn't planned on walking across the street to the pink cottage this evening, but his curiosity wouldn't have let him sleep. Too many questions had formed in his mind to rest without answers.

Lyla laughed out loud, grabbed him by the arm and said, "Get in here, you, Mr. Kennedy or Mr. Smith, whoever you are! Seems that I've been found out, but so have you. I recognized you as I sat at the stop light on Highway 70 the other day. Apparently, we are both in hiding at the Arcadia Retirement Village and I'm not sure why but please, I beg you, for my friend Betty's sake, to keep all of this our little secret."

Lyla offered Smith a glass of lemonade and a seat at a table in the breakfast nook. The room was small and cheery but most importantly, out of the line of sight of golf carts heading home down Sunset Lane. "So, I guess we begin with introductions? Although, I know who you are, and you know who am, I'll begin." Smith nodded a go ahead as he sipped his lemonade. "I really am Anne Knight!" Lyla began her story explaining that Anne and

Lyla are one in the same. She went on to briefly tell about her heart attack, leaving out the details of being found on her bathroom floor and asking for her lipstick. She concluded the tale with her own rendition of her dear publicist and assistant Beatrice Brown, known in the Village as Betty, begging and pleading with her to come hide in Arcadia to recover and gain her strength. It was with great dramatic flair that Lyla again stressed to Smith that for Beatrice's sake, no one must know their secret.

Smith laughed out loud and Lyla immediately took offense to his frivolity. "No, no, no, I don't take your heart-attack light-heartedly, nor your secret," he began in all seriousness, "but, my dear Miss Fontaine, let me tell my tale of woes and strokes and physical therapy!" Smith gave the details of his past as he told Lyla about his ties to the Arcadia antique shops and driving past the Putt-Putt on his way through town. He told her about Johnson's protests and introducing himself to Herb Lewis as the fellow that was hunted by commercial paparazzi and needing a break in his "later years," as Johnson so aptly put it.

Lyla listened wide-eyed at the strange similarities of their stories. Her daughter had taught her about the Sovereign God who loved the world so much He gave His Son, and all who followed Him did not live in a world of coincidences but in a great and mighty plan. "Mr. Smith," she began.

"Oh, please, drop the mister and just call me Smith," he interrupted.

"No, that's too revealing to who we really are. I must call you Leonard or Mr. Smith, and you must remember to address me as Anne Knight. Beginning tonight it's imperative that we stick to that plan." Smith agreed and she continued her thought, "I'll begin again, Leonard, I must ask a very personal question. Do you believe in God?"

The question shocked Smith and he simply nodded a 'yes'.

"Well, my daughter, the Reverend Beatrice Knight of the Wesley United Methodist Church of New Smyrna Beach, tells me there are no coincidences. This life is not serendipitous but part of God's plan. And may I be completely vulnerable in my next statement?"

Smith, still shocked by the actress's abruptness, could only manage a second nod to indicate 'yes'.

"Then, I will confess to you that tonight I prayed." Lyla didn't want to be so vulnerable that she would reveal her tears and her thoughts about the stars but she continued with a more vague statement, "I wonder, sir, if we are not experiencing some fortunate opportunity to be a part of something God has planned." With her flair for the dramatic Lyla waved her arms, "What if there is something more than therapy and refreshing for us to encounter here?"

Smith, still shocked but pleased with Lyla's insight responded in agreement, "Why my dear lady, that may be exactly why we have landed here together in Arcadia Retirement Village, incognito!"

They pledged their loyalty to one another's secrets and decided to keep their eyes and ears open to whatever heavenly assignment may lay ahead for them. They also agreed it would benefit their true identities if they did not appear to be in cahoots together so the two exchanged cell phone numbers and would call, text, and at least for the time being, only meet secretly, as needed.

They talked until nearly ten o'clock. The neighborhood grew quiet, and the street was clear of golf carts; the perfect time for Smith to return to his ocean blue cottage across the street. Lyla watched from the window for the safety of her new confidant as he crossed Sunset Lane before turning off her porch light.

Smith had just slipped inside when Lyla heard sirens wail. A police car rounded the bend and pulled into the drive four doors down. She wondered to herself if that was Ellwood's home or the cabin belonging to Esther and her husband? Betty's porch light broke the darkness and Lyla watched through her front window as Betty stepped into her front yard, followed by neighbors emerging from their homes, as well. Light after light flickered on revealing a parade of bathrobes, fuzzy slippers, and sweatpants gathering up and down the street.

Mrs. Willoughby stepped out with her hair wrapped in a bandana and a glass of wine in her hand. She waved to the others, "When the husband's cream-crackered he sleeps through any ruckus."

Betty left her yard and moved toward Lyla's. She held a cellphone to her ear as she walked. Lyla stepped outside to meet her on the steps and saw Smith open his front door across the street.

"Keep me informed, Dolores. Good night dear," Betty turned her cell to silent mode.

"Betty," Lyla gasped in disgust, "this would never happen in Beverly Hills. Neighbors mind their own business. They would never come out of their homes gawking at another's misfortune!" Lyla shuddered at the thought that one of her Beverly Hills neighbors could have seen her in the throes of her heart attack and reported her wailing in pain and wearing only a nighty to the press. It was bad enough the first responders had to see her, at least they were obligated to follow HIPAA regulations and were sworn to silence.

"You're in a new world Lyla. This is not Beverly Hills. In Arcadia, neighbors take care of one another. If a husband goes to the hospital, a neighbor may need to drive his wife. If someone has fallen, we will all keep an eye on that injured party to provide assistance in days to come. This isn't a world of news reporters and ugly headlines. This is an opportunity for Blanche to use her gift of gab, shall we say, and pass on the events to others so cards will be sent, dinners will be provided, and proper prayers will be prayed."

Lyla paused to think about what Betty had just said, she couldn't imagine that a group of people, strangers in a sense, would be willing to look out for one another so tenderly. She looked around and saw some figures gathering under the streetlamps near the police car. A couple of men at the corner could be heard discussing the matter, "At least they haven't sent an ambulance. It must not be too bad."

Betty agreed with the on-lookers, "Yes, looks like they aren't sending the EMT's, that's good news." She decided she would get back home since there was a nip in the air. "Sleep well, Ly... I mean Anne," she laughed and turned to maneuver the steps in time to see Smith wave from across the street and Lyla wave back.

"Put your hand down!" she scolded Lyla through clenched teeth.

Lyla returned the scolding, "Well, my goodness Betty Brown, I'm being neighborly! What a horrible way to respond to a friendly wave from a new 'Villager'."

"He is NOT a friend and NOT a neighbor, Lyla. He is NOT a human being. He is a REPORTER! I knew I recognized him the first time I saw him and then it dawned on me. He's an *investigative* reporter. I don't know who he works for, yet, but mark my words, I know he's here to get at you! You just leave that man to me. I'll take care of him!" Betty stomped her way home and looked back in Lyla's direction to make sure her door was shut and then in the direction of Smith's bungalow confirming all communication had ended.

Inside the pink cottage Lyla laughed her way to bed. Betty had Smith Kennedy pegged all wrong and there wasn't a thing she could do about it. The pact stood and secrets would remain secret until Lyla and Smith were sure of the plan they had found themselves in.

Chapter 11

By the time the warm Florida sun rose on Arcadia Retirement Village the following morning the story had reached the Club House, moved on to the pool area and was spreading through the mail room. The police were called to the Kornecky home because Sam had reported their E Z GO Golf cart missing.

The couple had stayed later than usual at the Club House the evening before as part of the clean-up crew. After, Sam took their schnauzer for an evening stroll and came home to see that the E Z GO was not parked in the drive where he parked it religiously, every night. He waved his arms at his wife, Coleen, who was chatting on her cell to Vicky, who lived two streets over. Coleen was deep in conversation about the new resident Anne Knight who was so pretty she had to have had "work done" and wondering if anyone had gotten any other details on the McCoy fellow and couldn't be bothered with Sam's gyrations, so he called the police on the land line and reported the golf cart missing.

When Officer Robertson arrived in the driveway Coleen was bidding Vicky goodbye and stepped out in the yard to hear her husband's words, "I park it right here every night, Robby."

Officer Robertson's first name was Robert. He was affectionately known as Robby to the Villagers since he spent an enormous amount of time with them. Arcadia Retirement Village had grown in leaps and bounds in quite a short span of time and as it grew so also did the number of calls to the Arcadia Police Department. Inevitably, once or twice or ten times a day someone misplaced a wallet or purse and became suspicious that a new cleaning lady had taken it, or the UPS man had lifted it from the table. Ovens and burners were left on causing fire alarms to blare summoning the police and first responders. Dogs were lost, the wind would blow down branches, a creak was heard in the night, or a garbage can would be left out on the curb too long causing neighbors to worry about the well-being of the owner and so the presence of the Arcadia Police was expected.

To help ease the burden of the calls, the Arcadia Police Department drew up a contract with the Arcadia Retirement Village in which they hired an officer to be paid by both entities. The residents were aware that this officer was available to strictly answer the calls from the Village and be first on sight to assess the situation.

Officer Robert Robertson, with the patience of a saint, received the assignment with joy.

"Who else could have moved it?" Robby asked Sam.

"Me," called Coleen from the porch. "I moved it around back to give it a good spraying off tomorrow morning and let it set in the sun to dry. I'm sure you'll find it out in the backyard."

"Sure enough," Officer Robby called from the back side of the cottage. "All's well, that ends well." That's how Officer Robby ended most of his calls to the Village because more times than not, they ended well. The lost purse was often found fallen into the back of a closet or the wallet had slipped between the couch cushions.

Sam responded as most Villagers do, "Aw geez, thank ya, Robby. I appreciate you coming out."

Officer Robertson was obligated to make reports for every call. For most he simply scribbled a few notes on the required forms then stacked them on his desk under a conch shell he had found on the Gulf a few years back. He often remarked how he hated to see a report with a name and address printed in the newspaper under the Police Blotter and when they were, he always seemed to share the embarrassment of the Village resident.

So, the next evening when Sam didn't see the golf cart in the driveway again, he didn't think much about it. He grumbled a little under his breath about Coleen moving it, but not until the following morning when he grabbed the keys to head to the pool for a late morning swim did he realize that no golf cart was to be found on the Kornecky property. "Coleen! Where'd you move it to now?" Sam bellowed at her as she ran the vacuum. She waved her arm begging him off until the job was done. When the machine was quiet, he asked again, "Where's the cart, Coleen?"

"Right outside Sam. You parked it in the drive when we came home from the card party last night," she offered.

"Well, it's not there and it's not out back. Where the heck did we leave it, now?"

The two took iced tea out to the patio to think about all the possibilities of where they could have left the cart and waited for Officer Robby to clock in for duty at noon. They had hoped to find it themselves avoiding any chance of his police car in their driveway twice in a week but by 12:30 p.m. they still hadn't located it and called.

"You don't need sirens, Robby, just stop by for a glass of iced tea when you get a free minute, will ya?" Sam asked.

It was mid-February as Smith reviewed the contractor's work on the 14th hole at the Putt- Putt Golf Course. He had given Crystal Bell creative license and was surprisingly pleased with the ideas she had developed that included a mechanical hippo and working windmill on the course, something she had seen on a family vacation in Louisiana. Her brightly colored designs would appeal to her peers and could already be seen taking shape from Highway 70. While she dealt with the painting contractors, Smith was free to work on the logistics of the physical needs of the course. New concrete was poured and leveled, and dark green turf replaced the peeling, faded AstroTurf that had been glued and re-glued to a deteriorating foundation.

As each hole was completed Smith would putt for hours focusing his vision and adjusting his weight from one foot to the other. He added a simulated driving range and would practice driving a golf ball on a screen at his choice of golf courses from all over the world. He began to feel the ease and comfort of the motion and follow through return. His physical therapist gladly spent extra time with Smith enjoying the change of pace from the in-office routine that many less fortunate stroke patients had to endure.

"What do you think, Crystal, will we be open for the rodeo this year?" Crystal rose to the occasion when Smith questioned her like a partner.

"I believe so, boss. Everything is comin' along. The painters turned out to be great guys. Paul, you know, Paul Patterson the owner of Patterson's Painting? Well, he said he hadn't ever taken orders from a teenager before but when he saw my designs, he got kinda nice. I think he was surprised that he liked 'em, boss. Anyway, he said they'll be done next week sometime if the weather stays nice. We have five weeks 'til the cowboys show up in town here. How about on your end? Will all eighteen holes be ready?"

Smith smiled at his junior manager, "From what they tell me it may be close, but we should be able to open a few days before the rodeo. That will give the good folks of Arcadia the chance to try out the course before it fills up with cowpokes!"

"Right on schedule, boss!" Crystal Bell was about to chatter on about the rodeo and the crowds that would descend on Arcadia for The All Florida Rodeo Championship, but Smith's phone buzzed. The caller ID announced that his son, Johnson, was calling in for his mid-week, 'dad-check.' Smith held up a pointer finger to Crystal and moved into his office.

His son's voice sounded relaxed, "Hello Dad. How are things coming along?"

"My business partner, Miss Bell, and I were just discussing a possible opening day, Johnson." Smith smiled knowing that Crystal had overheard. She had beamed at the contractors when Smith introduced her with that title.

"That's great, but what I meant is how are things with you, Dad, how is therapy progressing? And, I haven't seen you on the six o'clock news so apparently, you're still well hidden as Leonard Smith, the commercial king?" Johnson quipped.

"All's well on that front, Johnson, but boy do I have a story to tell you next time you visit. I have some rather interesting neighbors. When will you be back up this way?" Smith wasn't expecting his son for a week or so and wasn't in any particular hurry to have him arrive with the Highlander full of boxes. Johnson still wasn't sold on the idea of the Putt-Putt course and he always arrived in Arcadia ready to pack up the ocean blue bungalow and cart Smith home with him. Smith, however, was growing fond of this project, far more that he had expected he would. He wondered if having Lyla Fontaine as a neighbor swayed him at all; that was quite possible, but he was also a man who liked to finish what he had started. He wanted to see the Putt-Putt come to life, again. He was pleased with the way his therapy was progressing and that was a project he needed to finish, as well.

"About that, Dad," Johnson's voice took on a more serious tone, "I want to get up there, I need to get you back into the mainstream of life, for sure, but I just got off the phone with Frank Murphy. I think we could land that deal. He'd like to see our ideas on a course design outside of Dublin. If you're alright with it, I'd like to head to Ireland for a few weeks. I've thought about sending Bill on this assignment but I'm afraid we may lose the account if you or I don't go, in person."

Smith chuckled to himself and thought he could offer Johnson the expertise of Miss Crystal Bell, she had made quite the impression designing his golf course here in Arcadia, but instead offered his approval, "Godspeed, Son. I'd love to see you land that account! And, what a stunning course to work on. I will be fine here. I've made a few acquaintances and Miss Bell will drive me to any up-coming appointments that I need to keep."

"You got it, boss." Crystal called from the outer office. She didn't consider her listening in eavesdropping, more like company business with her partner.

With Johnson out of the country, Smith had full reign of his life again. He pulled in a long breath and exhaled a deep, contented sigh.

He thought he might text Lyla, just to keep in contact. He would hold to his promise and keep their lives a secret, but he was intrigued by her thoughts of the two of them being at the same place, at the same time, under similar circumstances. He would keep his distance, for now, but keep in touch and he could do that today by asking if she knew why the police cruiser was on Sunset Drive last night.

"Hello neighbor...enjoyed our meeting. Any news about the police?"

A few minutes later his phone sounded the familiar ding of a return message. It read, "False alarm... enjoyed our meeting as well. Hope to talk again."

Officer Robertson slowed to 15 miles per hour as he turned off Highway 70. He shook his head with a smile as he rolled past the Venus De Milo draped in her Valentine's Day get-up. His wife always asked him about his day at work, so he made a mental note to tell her about Venus's new trappings. He turned onto Sunset Lane and could see Sam and Coleen sitting on the cement patio under a bright red sun umbrella. Both were looking worried with iced tea in hand.

"Can I pour ya a glass, Robby?" Sam asked as Officer Robertson stepped out of the cruiser and said something unintelligible to the dispatcher as he spoke into the microphone clipped to his collar.

"Nope, you know I can't have the hard stuff on duty, Sam," Robby joked. He always had something light-hearted to say to ease any tension. He pulled up one of the lawn chairs and sat down facing Sam and Coleen, "What's going on, how can I help?" He leaned back in the chair under the cool shade of the umbrella.

"Well, we just can't find it again. We've misplaced the E Z Go."

Officer Robertson smiled reassuringly. He remembered as a kid in Minnesota that he often lost his winter coat, never maliciously but because Stevie Rowans, next in alphabetical order and subsequently on the seating chart, had one identical to his. One or the other of the two boys would invariably put on the wrong coat after school and wear it home, purely by accident. After the third mix up the boys caught on and just wore home whichever coat was left in the classroom. Robby was sure this was what happened with the Kornecky's E Z Go. Many of the Villagers had similar carts and it was an easy mistake to hop in the wrong one and head for home, especially after dark. Some of the residents had mounted flags to their rear seats to make their cart distinguishable after one embarrassed gal had driven the wrong golf cart home from the Piggly Wiggly stranding its owner and receiving a visit from Officer Robertson questioning her motives.

After the Piggly Wiggly incident, Robby mistakenly made the suggestion that golf cart owners take their keys out of the ignitions to avoid further mix ups but that presented a problem all its own, the result of which was countless calls concerning lost keys. Officer Robertson found himself searching multitudes of pockets in sweaters and jackets hanging in closets throughout the Village and restoring lost keys to stranded drivers. He finally conceded to the fact that there would always be a need to reunite Arcadia Villagers with their lost golf carts and he was man for the job.

"Have you retraced your steps? Called the folks you were at the party with last night?" he questioned in true detective fashion.

"That's what we did, first thing, but we just can't seem to find it, anywhere," Coleen said in a hushed voice not wanting the neighbors to think they were involved in another golf cart fiasco.

"Maybe if you could just keep a look out as you cruise the Village, Robby?" Sam leaned in and whispered.

"Of course, you got it. I'm sure it'll show up. All's well that ends well, you know." Officer Robertson pushed his chair back into its original position, and came back to the two before he walked to the police cruiser, "Listen, I'll write up a report," he said quietly, "but I won't file it with the chief quite yet. In the meantime, I'll take a good look around."

That was generally the pattern when it came to lost golf carts; a file sat on his desk under the conch shell before it was filed in the trash can when the cart was recovered.

The Korneckys gave him a thumbs up as he spoke into his collar again and backed out the drive. No one noticed Ellwood McCoy sitting in his recliner watching the scene unfold through the front window of his bungalow.

Chapter 12

"Beeeep! Beep! Beep!" sounded from the intersection of Mary Jean Drive and Highway 70 and Smith knew it came from the silver Porsche. Crystal looked out the office window to see it pull to a stop at the intersection. It was headed away from the Village and toward the antique shops in Arcadia. "Hey! That's Miss Anne and she's honkin' your way, boss!"

"It seems as though Miss Anne Knight and I met many years ago, Crystal." Smith continued, "We decided it must be a pretty small world and the Good Lord must have something in mind for us to accomplish here in Arcadia since we've had the pleasure of reconnecting again. What do you think?" He delighted in listening to Crystal Bell expound on her philosophies of life. Although young and naïve, she had a bit of wisdom and humor that would often ring true in the moment.

"Well, if you really want to know, boss, I'd love, love, love to tell ya! I've just been bustin' to give ya my advice on that one," she bubbled from outside his office, her voice muffled and distant.

"I'm all ears," Smith said as he turned around to find her leaning through the door waving back to the honking silver Porsche.

She pulled herself back into the room. "The two of you are somethin' different, not crazy different or bad different, but a good kinda different." Smith knew what Crystal meant. He and Lyla Fontaine had a unique past that caused them both to think differently, to see the world with broader vision. They even carried themselves differently than most others. He noticed that distinctiveness as he watched the Willoughbys and Ellwood McCoy come to the microphone in the Club House. There was nothing wrong with them, they just seemed to blend into the crowd. Lyla, on the other hand, had the opposite effect. There was an air about her. When she stepped into a room, she commanded the space with her presence.

Crystal continued, "Well, you two are just kinda like a couple of magnets and folks seem to get drawn to ya and caught by ya. You know what I mean, boss? You're like from a whole different planet and I sure wish I knew what planet it is 'cuz I think I'd like to visit there someday! Some planet in the stars far away from Arcadia!" she giggled.

As they pulled away from the traffic light, Betty scowled at Lyla, "Why in the world did you beep there? What do you think you're doing? You don't know what I know about that man, Lyla. You have no idea."

"Don't worry so, dear," Lyla consoled her friend on their way to Arcadia's Historic District. "The first lesson we both learned in Hollywood was to keep your friends close and your enemies closer." She hoped this would console Betty until the truth could be made clear.

Betty harrumphed and shook her head, "I've spent my career protecting you, Miss Lyla Fontaine, I think I know my job. Now just listen to me, that man is not here in Arcadia Retirement Village by accident. It's part of a plan and you must remain diligent about your identity. Do you understand me?"

Lyla smiled and thought to herself, *If you only knew, Betty, if you only knew!*

Lyla parked the Porsche and found two quarters in her Coach clutch to drop in the meter. Betty and Lyla had decided to take a stroll through some of the antique shops that lined Maple Street in downtown Arcadia. They talked a bit about Hollywood and the latest gossip concerning their generation of stars, but it wasn't as juicy as it had been in years past. Now their talk consisted of hospital visits resulting from broken hips rather than hotel visits leading to broken relationships. But the two old friends linked arm-in-arm strolled up and down aisles and giggled over old stories and memories.

Some of the antique knick-knacks conjured up images of old sets and bad scripts. Betty perused a stack of vinyl albums recorded by great musical artists back in their glory years and Lyla eyed the lead glass goblets and etched tumblers. Coming to the end of a line of dusty shelves in one of the drearier stores, the two were greeted by a big woman sitting at an antique cash register. She was busy fanning herself with a folded newspaper, the small gusts causing the dust on the shelves behind her to swirl. Anne felt beads of perspiration forming on her forehead. Both she and Betty had grown tired and silent in the afternoon heat. Nodding to the fanning woman, they moved outside and walked the city block to a wooden bench at the corner of a little diner. There they sat and rested, leaning against the old brick wall under a spreading magnolia tree as cars with Arcadians slowly drove past.

In their silence, they became aware of a man's hushed, gruff voice around the corner of the building. It was a one-sided conversation, someone talking on their cell, but it grabbed the attention of both ladies. Betty slowly lifted her pointer finger to her lips and Lyla nodded in agreement.

"Yup, got it, last night. Haven't heard nothing about the police bein' called.... E Z Go, about a year old.... Nope ain't got it delivered yet, we'll get it there tonight...."

Lyla and Betty listened wide-eyed until they realized the conversation was coming to an end. Betty began to panic and raised her hands and her eyebrows in a questioning motion, worried they may be found out. Lyla, remembering her Bond days, sprang into action and quietly tiptoed a few feet down the sidewalk, shuffled her feet then called out in a cheery voice, "The store is just around this corner, dear! Let's have a quick peek inside!"

They heard what seemed to be the footsteps of a rather large man thud quickly down the sidewalk toward the far corner of the building. Lyla leaned past the bricks in time to see the back of a brown and orange flannel shirt with the sleeves cut off, a pair of old blue jeans and worn out work boots turning into an ally.

"Oh, dear me, oh dear," was all that Betty could utter as the two ladies hurried one block down Maple Street to the Porsche.

Bond girl, Lyla, kept her wits and jumped into action. She slipped into the driver's seat and started the ignition. Betty barely had her leg in the door before Lyla pulled from the curb. She turned left rather than right which would have been a direct route back to Highway 70.

"Where are you going? Lyla? What do you think you're doing?" Betty sputtered, still fumbling with the seat belt. "Slow down, you're an old woman, would you please drive like it!" She practiced the deep breathing she learned in yoga class to slow her heart rate as Lyla pumped the brake for the red traffic light ahead. As the two neared the intersection an old grey pickup truck made a right-hand turn under the light in front of them. A bare elbow and forearm protruded from the driver's window. The women only had moments to survey the scene but capping the driver's bicep was what was left of a frayed, orange, and brown plaid sleeve.

"We're going to follow that truck, Betty. Get out a pen and paper and write down the license plate number. I'll stay behind and trail him until you're ready, then I'll speed up and get close enough for you to get a good look." Lyla turned the corner onto Old Oak and caught a glimpse of the pickup ahead at the stop sign. As he pulled forward, Lyla put on her blinker and turned to follow him. "He won't notice us if I stay behind him."

Betty nodded dutifully until she realized they were hardly inconspicuous. "Lyla, are you kidding me? What are you thinking? Two old ladies can't follow a man in a pickup unnoticed in a Porsche!"

Lyla threw a disgusted look in her direction, "Just watch, love. I learned this on set, he'll never know."

The pickup turned north onto Highway 70 and Lyla pushed through the intersection and under the yellow light just as it flashed red. Betty stifled a scream and held her eyes tightly shut. In her panic she threw her hands to the roof of the passenger's seat and slammed her Prada's into the floor. As they rounded a curve, she leaned into the door and clung to the arm rest to steady herself.

"Betty, dear, get ahold of yourself," Lyla ordered.

"I wish I could!" Betty hollered, "I'm white knuckled on the door handle, Lyla! Thank the Lord this is not a convertible or you would have rolled me onto the curb back there!"

The truck pulled ahead in the line of traffic, Lyla changed lanes and pulled out in front of a moving van. She pressed the gas pedal a little closer to the floor as they sped past the entrance to the Arcadia Retirement Village and Venus De Milo. "Get ready, Betty, we're closing in on him. You'll need to write the number down."

Seeing they were on a straight-away, Betty let go of the door, found her purse, and fumbled for a pen. Her cell phone fell into her lap and her glasses slid to the floor under her seat.

Lyla changed lanes again and pulled in behind the pickup, "Okay Betty, get the number!"

"I can't find my glasses, Lyla, I can't read the plate."

"You certainly wouldn't have been much help to James Bond," Lyla complained. She squinted through her sunglasses, "just write this down." With no paper to be found, Betty released the door handle, opened her hand, and scribbled the letters and numbers onto her palm as Lyla called them out: "G R G 7 5 5 9"

The pickup's right blinker popped on. Up ahead was a gravel turn-off that led under a big wooden sign mounted between two wooden posts. Lyla read, "*Low Land Palms Cattle Ranch.*" She maneuvered into the passing lane and slowed down as the truck and driver began to make a sharp right turn. Betty reached for her phone, pulled up her camera and held it to the window as they passed. She steadied her hand working to focus the camera without her glasses when the man in the flannel shirt turned and looked directly at her. He snarled and she dropped the phone in fear. A wave of sweat and nausea came over her, "Oh Lyla, let's get out of here," she whispered as she began her deep breathing again. The two vehicles parted.

Lyla and Betty looked at each other with jaws dropped. "Oh dear, oh dear, Lyla, what if he comes after us? What did we get ourselves into?" Betty thought out loud.

For a split-second Lyla wondered if she should have simply minded her own business and not channeled her inner Bond persona, but it was too late now. There was a moment of contemplative silence as the ladies turned the Porsche back in the direction of the Village. Lyla wasn't exactly sure what she had heard during that conversation back on the street but one thing she was sure she understood; a person of detestable character was telling someone else with obviously poor character that he had taken something that didn't belong to him. She remembered it was an easy-going something that was about a year old. And if her memory served her correctly, it was something with value that may even concern the police.

Lyla spoke quietly as if she might be heard by someone other than Betty, "What do you think that phone call was all about?"

"Something is amiss, Lyla. I'm not sure what, but whatever it is, we're witnesses to wrongdoing, even if we don't know what it is."

"Betty," Lyla worried, "Do you think, this involves dognapping? I've heard about black market puppy sales. One of the nightly news broadcasts ran a story about it while I was recovering in the hospital. If it's an issue on the West Coast, maybe it's happening here, as well."

Betty stared at Lyla in silence, maintaining her deep breathing.

Lyla explained, "That awful man said he took something easy-going, about a year old. Think about it, Betty, what could he have taken that would be a year old and easy-going that he could deliver tonight? I can only think of one thing: a puppy.

Getting light-headed Betty closed her eyes but continued to listen in silence, taking in what Lyla was suggesting.

"A sweet little pup, yes, this awful man has pilfered a one-year-old puppy, possibly of great value. One of those designer dogs! My neighbor in Beverly Hills spent thousands of dollars on a tiny little thing that she carried in her purse, which may I clarify, I found ridiculous. But, I find it even more horrifying that Mr. Flannel Shirt, depraved as he is, could have taken a pup from its owner, who is most likely sick with worry, to sell in one of those puppy mills I've read about!"

Betty bit her lip and squeezed her eyes tightly shut. "Oh dear, oh dear, poor thing, poor, poor little thing. I've read about designer dogs, they are highly intelligent creatures, easy to train and quite valuable."

Lyla agreed, "At least we have the license plate. I believe we should call Officer Robertson, immediately."

Betty began to breathe easier as they drove past the giant aqua-marine seashell and the Venus De Milo. She looked at her sweaty palm, smeared and glistening from perspiration. The letters and numbers had run together. She could only make out the G, an R, and what she thought was a 9.

It was a relief to be back in safety behind the stucco wall. Lyla and Betty, both wide-eyed stared straight ahead unaware of the grey pickup that slowly passed the entrance of the Arcadia Retirement Village as they turned onto Sunset Lane.

Officer Robertson picked up the phone at the station. "Yes, Ms. Brown, thank you, I'm happy I'm here in the office to take your call. Now how can I help you?"

Betty began the tale of her afternoon with Anne Knight in downtown Arcadia. She told Officer Robertson of the unsettling conversation they had overheard. "Oh, no Robby, we weren't eavesdropping, no, we just overheard this fellow mumbling around the corner. He said that he had something that didn't belong to him. And we got a look at him. He had on flannel and blue jeans and he drove a dreadfully noisy, old pick-up truck."

Lyla waited intently when Betty paused while Officer Robertson said something on the other end of the line.

Betty continued, "No Robby, we wouldn't get in the way of the police department's work, we're just trying to help stop a crime. We think this derelict has taken, well, a valuable dog, a puppy, perhaps. He said it was about a year old and it was easy-going, and he would deliver it at night..."

Robby put his pencil down and drummed the table, "Ms. Brown, I'm not sure you have enough evidence for me to follow up on this call, but if you hear of anyone missing their dog I'll gladly get right on it."

"Don't you want to know where we followed him to, Officer? He drove to..."

Officer Robertson interrupted, "Ms. Brown, please leave any detective work to me. It's not safe to be following anyone that you might think is suspicious. But you can call me anytime, okay?"

"Officer, I hope that you understand that this is a very serious matter," Betty sounded disappointed at his lack of interest.

Robby answered her as encouragingly as he could, "I will keep my eyes open and my ears turned up, Ms. Brown. We'll be on the lookout for dog-nappers. All's well that ends well, you know."

"Yes, I know," she sighed and pushed the end call button on her cell.

Chapter 13

Smith parked his golf cart in the carport connected to the ocean blue bungalow and glanced across the street hoping Lyla Fontaine or Anne, as he had to remember to address her, would be sitting outside on her front porch. It certainly wouldn't look suspicious for one neighbor to *nonchalantly* give a friendly wave then stroll across the street to visit another neighbor sitting outside enjoying the sunset. He had noted that other neighbors often made a whole evening of strolling the streets, stopping from house to house. A few of the women on Sunset Lane made it a habit to *nonchalantly* bring him cookies and desserts when he happened to be in his front yard so a stroll to visit Anne Knight would be completely natural, he reasoned.

Unfortunately, Lyla was nowhere in sight, but Betty Brown was in the front lawn of her yellow cottage pulling dandelions along the curb. She hadn't been especially friendly to Smith and it was quite evident to him that she made every effort to avoid him. They had exchanged only a few pleasantries since he had moved into the Village, but Betty was always quick to end every conversation that moved beyond the local weather report. Smith knew a back-story lurked behind Betty's scowl, her life a secret much like Lyla's and his, and not knowing the extent of her story was getting the best of him. He made up his mind; he would *nonchalantly* reassure her that he was friend, not foe.

Smith had grown tired of his cane and in a moment of genius, he exchanged it for a putter from his golf bag. He looked far less debilitated when carrying the golf club rather than the four-pronged, hospital issued monstrosity. Employing the hospital equipment, the populace outside of the stucco-walled, retirement village found it reasonable to assume that his faculties were substandard. When seeing the elder man carrying the cane, non-residents of the Village behaved, whether consciously or unconsciously, as though the cane had somehow dulled his hearing and dimmed his eyesight and gave approval for complete strangers to refer to him as "dear" or even worse, "sweetie".

Smith Kennedy felt his virility melt down his body and spill out through his shoes every time he leaned against the cane and often thought of drawing it up like a sword, thrusting the prongs into the chests of thirty and forty-somethings who opened the door for him or offered to load his groceries into his Club Cab.

He understood the kindness in their gestures but knew they did not understand his need to be independent.

His mind was keen and thoughtful, and well on his way to recovery, he didn't have a problem with his faculties, however, he did have a problem with offensive assumptions. He was growing tired of strangers patronizing him and the age-profiling that assumed him to be weak or incompetent. So, he brilliantly exchanged the cane for the putter and immediately found carrying the club turned conversation into a hushed whisper as if someone were about to attempt a five-foot putt out on the back nine. Chatting no longer centered on convalescing but turned to the very thing that drove his motivation to heal and bolstered his confidence. Any conversation spent discussing the strokes taken on the golf course rather than rehashing the debilitation of the stroke that sent him to the hospital, brought him one step closer to being Smith Kennedy again.

So, with the putter in hand, Smith *nonchalantly* headed in Betty's direction.

"Don't you dare come one step closer, mister!" Betty held her dandelion-plucker pointed in Smith's direction as he reached the edge of her manicured lawn. She pushed herself up to her feet, "I know who you are. You have got some nerve, disguised as Mr. Putt-Putt, taking advantage of, of... you know who...in her vulnerability!"

Smith responded to Betty's unwarranted attack by grabbing the head of the putter and swinging the shaft upward pointing it directly at her in self-defense! "Wait a minute, lady!" his voice escalating, "I don't know what you're talking about, but you need to drop the weapon!"

Smith's every move was carefully scrutinized from behind the curtains in the cottages and bungalows of the widows and divorcees up and down Sunset Lane. As the two stood face-to-face, dandelion-plucker-to-putter Norma Jean quickly called the Arcadia Police department in an attempt to spare Mr. Smith's life. She put in a request for Officer Robertson to come quickly and de-escalate the trouble that was brewing. "I'm afraid Mr. Smith is going to get hurt. Ms. Brown is threatening him with a weapon of some sort. Please, hurry," she whimpered to the dispatcher, worried for his well-being.

"YOU! YOU REPORTER!" Betty hissed at Smith, "Just go back under the rock you crawled out from and leave Ly...," she stopped herself before she said it, "JUST LEAVE!" As the stand-off continued the two kept their voices at a low growl. Hearing aids could be heard squealing inside cottages nearby as the neighbors appeared in windows and turned them up, full volume picking up distance frequencies.

"You have no idea what you're talking about Betty. I'm NOT a reporter. I'm not here to reveal..." Smith hushed his voice to a whisper and dropped the end of his golf club to the ground, "I know you don't believe me, but I'm here for the same reason you are Betty. Now, put down the plucker, lower your voice and," Smith was jarred by the sound of a siren turning off Highway 70 and entering Arcadia Retirement Village.

"Excuse me! Hellooo, you two..." Looking past the dandelion-plucker, Smith saw startled faces peering from the windows in the cottages around them. Lyla was leaning out her opened door waving her arms to shush them. She motioned both to come into the pink cottage and get out of the street.

As the cruiser drove past, the three stood on Lyla's front porch and waved and smiled at Officer Robertson. Lyla opened the screen door and all three *nonchalantly* walked in together.

With pursed lips, Lyla's eyes darted between the two. "Well," she paused and placed French-manicured fingertips on the shoulder of each friend and took the stance of a referee at a boxing match, "What was that all about, you two? You were hardly being inconspicuous."

"Anne, I don't want this reporter to divulge your where-abouts. I'm just trying to protect you, Anne." Betty raised her dandelion-plucker to Smith again. He stepped back, putter in hand, ready to defend himself from her attack.

"I'm NOT a reporter!" protested Smith.

"Alright, both of you listen," Lyla said calmly, "it's time we all understand; the three of us have found ourselves in the Arcadia Retirement Village in a very odd set of circumstances."

There was a knock at Lyla's door. The police cruiser had pulled into Lyla's drive behind her Porsche. Officer Robby let the engine run while he stood outside the screen.

"Oh, come in, dear," Lyla motioned to the officer to step into the cottage, which was now a bit crowded as the four of them stood in the small living room. "Hello, Officer. Let me introduce myself, I'm Anne Knight," Lyla extended her hand. "I've seen you cruise the Village; I'm so very thankful for your service. Can I get you a lemonade?"

"Hello Ma'am," Robby respectfully removed his hat and shook her hand, "I'm Officer Robertson but the folks in the Village just call me Robby. Thanks for the offer of a lemonade but I can't drink the hard stuff on duty," he said with a smile. "I just got a call about a squabble with possible weapons involved. I couldn't imagine an argument like that here in Arcadia Retirement Village, but I came right away. One of the other Villagers said the altercation was taking place out in the street."

"Oh Robby," Betty began, "I was just showing Mr. Smith my dandelion-plucker. This one right here." She waved it around like a dagger and laughed. "And he was showing me this beauty of a golf club of his," Betty and Smith re-enacted the scene, this time with pleasant smiles and laughter.

"Ms. Brown," Robby tipped his head in her direction, "When I heard the complaint involved you, I knew there had to be a mistake, ma'am."

Betty smiled, "Thank you, Robby. I'm glad you know me so well, dear."

Robby turned to Smith, "I never thought I would meet you in person, sir. I know this is hardly professional, while I'm on a call, but can I have your autograph, Mr. Kennedy? I've been wanting to stop by the Putt-Putt to introduce myself, but I wasn't sure what to say. I'm sure you get that all the time."

Betty was shocked. He had lied to her! This Leonard Smith character was not who he said he was. *Reporters!* She thought to herself. She wanted to spit on his shoes and would have if she wasn't standing in the living room of the pink cottage rented by the great Lyla Fontaine. Reporter or not, it just wouldn't be appropriate at that moment. She decided spitting on this man's shoes would wait until a later time.

Smith faked a sheepish smile, "I'm sorry, Officer, I'm sorry to disappoint you but I'm Mr. Smith, Leonard Smith. You know, I get that all the time. I don't see the resemblance, but I'm often confused with the golfer." Smith hated lying to an officer of the law. He promised himself, if the truth were to ever come out, he would apologize to Officer Robby.

"Well, I'll be!" Robby exclaimed, "You're a dead ringer, buddy. And I heard you're the guy that's reopening the Putt-Putt. Pretty uncanny!" Robby took off his police cap and rubbed his head. "Well, I'm going to write this up as a misunderstanding, folks."

"All's well that ends well," he called as he left the pink cottage and started for his cruiser. Then he mumbled into the microphone on his collar, intelligible to only the dispatcher, "There's something going on here that we need to keep an eye on."

The three remained silent inside Lyla's cottage until Officer Robertson had closed his car door and was backing out onto Sunset Lane.

"LIAR! You are despicable Mr. Smith or whoever you are," Betty raised her dandelion-plucker again and shook it at Smith.

Lyla could take no more, it started with a chuckle that rolled into a hoot followed by a snort! She burst into laughter and laughed louder and harder than she had in years. Gasping for breath she dropped on the love seat, doubled over. Betty panicked and ran for Lyla's heart pills in her medicine cabinet.

Lyla gasped again and tried to catch her breath, "Oh that was rich!" She sputtered between hoots, "I haven't laughed like that in years. Betty, you are such a wonderful friend, it's time you heard the truth." She turned to Smith, "She must know, may I tell her?"

"Please," Smith begged, "but first disarm her, would you? Put that dandelion-plucker far out of reach!"

Lyla patted the cushion next to her and motioned for Betty to sit beside her on the loveseat. "Beatrice, this is Smith Kennedy, the Pro-golfer who won the masters the year I filmed *James Bond Undercover Belgrade.* I even believe he may have won it at least once since then, but he is certainly not a reporter, Beatrice. Smith experienced a stroke a few months back, about the same time as I had my heart attack. He found his way here to Arcadia Retirement Village much like you and me. He is trying to live anonymously, again, much like you and me, and use his time of physical therapy to regain strength. Fortunately for the Arcadians, while doing so, he is re-decorating that cute little Putt-Putt golf course.

"Well, not so much redecorating," he corrected, "as rebuilding or renovating or restoring." Redecorating was what Lyla Fontaine might do to a Putt-Putt course; Smith Kennedy would restore it.

"Yes," Lyla gave a patronizing nod, "Mr. Kennedy is here to 'restore' himself while doing whatever he is doing to the little golf game and he is avoiding the press, Beatrice. I could hardly believe it myself as we shared our stories, but it's true. We are three peas in a pod, hiding! Thank you for protecting me so fiercely, dear, but there is no need to protect me from Smith Kennedy AKA Leonard Smith."

"Oh, Mr. Smith, or Mr. Kennedy, I knew I had seen your face before, I just assumed it was from the news," Betty said apologetically. She put her head in her hands and began to chortle, then from deep within came a belly laugh, loud and long, "I was convinced you were a reporter, Mr. Kennedy, can you believe it?" Her giggles continued to bubble out.

"Well, I suppose you did see him on the news, you've just remembered him on the wrong side of the anchor desk, dear." Lyla proffered.

The three formed a pact to keep their identities a secret. Beatrice would continue her life as Betty Brown, Villager. Lyla was feeling rested and would begin preparations to return to Beverly Hills after keeping her promise to her daughter to attend Easter Sunday Service at Betts's church. Smith would finish the Putt-Putt golf course project and turn it over to the capable Crystal Bell to manage before he returned home to Orlando to assist Johnson on the Ireland project.

All's well that ends well, so they say.

Chapter 14

"Arcadia Police Department, may I help you?"

"Could you send Officer Robertson over to 241 Magnolia Lane? We've had a little mishap; we're looking for our golf cart."

It was that time of year, again. During the Spring season, the calls to the Arcadia Police Department concerning missing golf carts at the Retirement Village seemed endless. As the temperature rose, the Villagers would take advantage of the warmer evenings to walk, rather than ride, to and from their destinations. It was good exercise for the legs, but the brains would often forget whether they had driven or walked or where they had last parked.

Robby recounted last Tuesday when Greta Copanhaugen was sure she had left her cart in the pool area all night but couldn't find it the following morning. Fortunately, after a call to Officer Robertson, he found it parked at a cottage on Happy Dale Lane where a group had gathered the night before to watch reruns of the old Andy Griffith show.

Avoiding the use of his lights and siren at the Wilson's request, Robby turned off Highway 70 and drove past Venus De Milo now adorned in a green top hat with a glittery cutout shamrock fastened to the front. He still hadn't filed the missing golf cart report for the Kornecky's. The chief had urged him to wait another day or two, and Robby reassured Sam and Coleen he was sure the cart would turn up somewhere before too long.

Esther and Jim were waiting and welcomed him in. "Can I get you something to drink, Officer Robby?" Esther offered.

"Nope, no thanks Esther, can't have the hard stuff while I'm on duty, you know." They all smiled. "Now what can I help you with?"

"Well," Jim began, "Seems as though we're the latest couple of old folks that have misplaced a golf cart."

Jim and Esther had spent the evening at the Club House playing in a Euchre tournament. They hadn't fared well, and Jim was quite unhappy about their performance but not wanting to appear to be a sore loser he decided he wouldn't be the first to leave.

He was relieved that within minutes of their disastrous defeat, David Willoughby gave a rather large, exaggerated yawn and headed for the door. He looked back at Susan who was still sitting at one of the Euchre tables, "I'm feelin' a bit knackered and need a kip, love. Are you comin' with me or stayin' in the game?"

Susan shook her head at the folks at the table and excused herself, "Oh that David, he's not going to wait for me. I'll be hanging on to the cart like a fire wagon if I don't skedaddle along," she laughed and followed David out the door.

"Hang on tight Susan," the others laughed. The kind-hearted neighbors were feeling badly for the Willoughbys. Their children had made no attempt to visit the couple since they relocated in the Village all the way from London. The watchful neighbors on Sunset Lane discussed the unfortunate situation and took it upon themselves to cheer the Willoughbys by inviting them to be a part of the Tuesday evening Euchre tournaments.

As Susan and David headed for the Club House door, Jim took the opportunity to follow them out and sulked home. Esther, who was not nearly as competitive as her husband and loved sharing a cup of decaf and a piece of pie with friends, lingered behind and accepted a ride home with another couple. When she arrived, she realized the golf cart wasn't in the carport.

"I thought I drove it home from the Club House tonight but I was feeling mighty foul after being the first couple out of the tournament so my mind was elsewhere, you know what I mean? Esther says she rode home with the neighbors after dessert, and, by golly, when she got home, we couldn't find the darn thing," Jim explained.

"Okay, no problem, don't you worry about it," Officer Robertson was always encouraging. "I'll write up a report and keep a look out for it. I'll just need a description."

"It's a hum-dinger, an E Z Go with an Ohio License plate on the back. We took the old one off the car up north and fixed it to the cart, so we'd know it was ours. You remember when we got mixed up with the Jackson's and took their cart home from the pool? They reported it stolen and we thought you might haul us off to jail when everyone discovered we were the thieves." Jim laughed out loud as he remembered the mix up. "I figure something like that has happened again."

"I'm sure you're right, Jim. Now don't you worry, Esther, we'll get this taken care of and get the right golf cart back to the right owner. All's well that ends well, you know." Officer Robertson returned to the cruiser.

A police car in the Village, sirens or not, never went unnoticed. As always, a few neighbors had assembled under the streetlight and many stood on their porches in robes and slippers. Susan Willoughby emerged from her home with a glass of wine and waved with her free hand, "David was knackered, out like a light you know. Is everybody okay down there?"

The crowd under the streetlight gave a thumbs up and someone shouted, "Anybody seen Jim and Esther's E Z Go?" Laughter followed as a few voices could be heard saying something about Jim's "some-timers" and that they'd look in the morning. The group dispersed relieved to know nothing was really amiss.

Ellwood McCoy took in the whole scene from the shadows of his carport. He nodded and mumbled "Yup" as residents passed his home and waved good night.

Lyla stepped from her front porch and made the walk across the street to Betty's cottage, this time. Dolores had phoned Betty as soon as she heard the call come across the police scanner she installed in her bedroom. Dolores always slept better knowing she would be made aware every time an emergency vehicle was dispatched to the Village. A list of phone numbers to call, depending on the street address in need of Officer Robby, was kept on her nightstand and she was quite efficient to follow up for any and all pertinent information. Betty was her contact for Sunset Lane.

Officer Robertson spoke into the microphone on his lapel notifying the dispatcher that he would make one more pass through the Village before he headed back to the office to fill out the paperwork. He turned toward the Club House to check the parking lot one more time then left Arcadia Retirement Village driving past the giant seashell and the Venus De Milo.

Chapter 15

Smith was pleased with the work the contractors had completed at the Putt-Putt. With fresh concrete poured, new turf laid, and the double loopty-loop installed on hole 7, the course would be ready for the grand opening just in time for the rodeo. Brightly colored paint was being applied to the exterior office walls and already drawing attention from passers-by. The Village was abuzz with daily updates from Piggly Wiggly shoppers peering across the parking lot as the town residents counted the days until the grand opening.

A team of high school students were hired to man the golf course after school and on weekends by junior manager Crystal Bell, with Smith's approval. She had suggested adding a snack stand but time was running short for permits to be granted from the DeSoto county health department so a plea was made for food truck venders offering the opportunity to set up for grand opening weekend and during rodeo week in the Putt-Putt parking lot. Crystal was especially excited when

Macho Nacho Mexican Cuisine agreed to offer their tacos and burritos in a bright orange truck that donned an inflatable, giant sombrero. *Smooth Southern Ice-Cold Treats* signed-on to park next to *Macho Nacho* and serve a variety of frozen delights giving the putt-putters a superb selection of food truck dining.

Smith sat at his desk and jotted down a few more "to-dos" on his endless list. Movement caught his peripheral vision and he leaned in his chair to look out the window. The silver Porsche pulled into a parking spot next to his Club Car. He stood to meet Lyla and Betty but as he reached the door, he could see the two still seated in the car in thoughtful conversation. Deciding it would be best to delay until he was sure it was safe for him to approach them, Smith waited. It was possible that Ms. Brown might, at any moment, revert back to her original poor opinion of him and he wasn't up to facing her dandelion-plucker this afternoon.

Betty unbuckled her seat belt and repositioned herself in the passenger seat to look directly at Lyla, "I believe you're on to something. I've wondered the same thing but pushed the thought away afraid I may be overreacting," she confessed. "But Lyla, there are just too many misplaced golf carts in the Village."

Living out movie scripts and playing the part of a Bond Girl often caused Lyla's imagination to get the best of her. Back in Beverly Hills she would lay in bed on sleepless nights and envision some hoodlum disarming the alarm system, scaling the wall around her property, and finding an open second story window into her home after maneuvering across the pergola.

However frightening that seemed, the thought never occurred to her to worry about her physical safety or welfare. She had been the girl-next-door, America's sweetheart, beloved by her fans and now, though she hated to admit it, loved by her fans' children and grandchildren. But love her or not, she was sure there were plenty who envied her collection of jewelry and gemstones from around the world. She wouldn't put it past some awful thug to try to heist them from her safe.

"Beatrice, on occasion I find myself concerned that my overactive imagination may lead me down an unwarranted path, but since the day we overheard that unsightly gangster on the phone, and followed his truck, I've kept my eyes and ears open. I can honestly say I wasn't sure what easy-going 'thing'," she made the sign for quotation marks in the air as she said the word thing, "he took or what 'thing'," she made the sign a second time to stress her point, "we wanted Robby to look for but-"

"E Z Go! Lyla, E Z Go!" Betty whispered. "Lyla, that's it!" Betty put her hands over her mouth in astonishment, "It's not something easy going that is missing, it's an E Z Go golf cart!"

"Yes, Betty, that is exactly the conclusion I was about to share with you." Lyla often used too many words of explanation before she wound her way to the point and this time Betty beat her there. "And, if you think about it," she continued, "there is a pattern. A couple goes to the Club House together in a golf cart and leaves separately, and voila, the cart comes up missing. Sometimes it seems to be recovered but most times, not."

Betty turned to her friend, "Oh, Lyla, you are definitely on to something."

Bam! Bam!

Both ladies jumped in their seats and let out a shriek!

Smith, tired of waiting in the office, made his way to the front of the Porsche and tapped lightly on the hood. He hadn't meant to frighten them, but his light touch echoed loudly into their perilous thoughts.

"I'm sorry ladies, didn't mean to give you a fright like that," he smiled apologetically.

This time, Lyla didn't return his apology with her signature smile but instead, looked him solemnly in the eyes, "Smith meet us at my cottage tonight, seven o'clock. Both Beatrice and I have made an observation that we wish to share with you. We may need your help." Lyla was adamant and Smith determined then and there that he wouldn't disappoint his two newly claimed comrades in arms.

At 7:00 p.m. sharp, Smith knocked on Lyla's screen door. "Come in, Smith. We've been waiting for you. Lemonade?"

"Yes, thank you, I'd love some. Whew, it's a warm one out there tonight. You know this Florida heat. It's only going to get hotter and muggier," Smith said as he reached for the icy glass Lyla was holding out.

"Stop with the pleasantries, you two," Betty interrupted. She pointed her finger at Smith, and he flashed back to the dandelion-plucker incident, "Smith Kennedy, I did not want to share this with you, but Lyla insisted. She thinks your input will be beneficial. That, Sir, is yet to be determined." Betty turned her finger on Lyla and in business-like fashion continued, "Lyla, I think I should do the talking as you are prone to embellishment."

"I suppose, but I will interject the important details you will most likely leave out," Lyla harrumphed.

Smith grinned. The two women had a history that granted them the freedom to speak bare truth to one another and a friendship that would accept it. He almost felt like an intruder as he sat down at the small table in the breakfast nook, "My curiosity needs quenched ladies, what is going on?"

Betty pulled out her notebook. She had jotted down the course of events in bullet points. At the top of the page was written *Missing Golf Carts*. She began recounting the night after the New Neighbor Party and the Kornecky's missing E Z Go. Betty explained further that Dolores had also informed her that a few days after the Kornecky incident, William and Selma Bougher had reported their cart missing. They had enjoyed dinner with friends at the Golf Club but soon after dessert Selma felt a headache coming on, so she walked home to get some fresh air. Later that evening, not finding the cart in the parking lot, William walked home as well. It wasn't until morning that the two realized their Polaris was nowhere to be found.

A couple of Sundays back, Harry and Missy Jones couldn't locate their Yamaha as they were getting ready for church and had to hitch a ride with other parishioners. However, their golf cart was later discovered at the Willoughby's. David had driven it home and parked it in the backyard of their bungalow.

When Susan arrived at the Club House that Sunday morning to have coffee with neighbors, Blanche began to spew the latest Village gossip. She had heard that someone else said they had talked to an acquaintance on Sunset Lane who was sitting outside on Saturday evening and spotted David driving the wrong golf cart home down the lane. Susan was on her cell immediately, "David, did you drive a golf cart home last night?" She paused listening to his response, then continued, "Well, love, I drove a cart home myself, so apparently, one of us has pocketed the wrong keys! I do believe we are in possession of the golf cart that belongs to the Jones's." She shook her head and sighed, "That man is a few quid short sometimes. I don't know what I'm going to do with him."

"Honest mistake. 'Yamaha was returned immediately.'" Betty read from her bullet points.

Sylvia Watson from the other side of the Village drove to the pool on Tuesday afternoon for water aerobics. After exercising, the girls in the class changed in the cabana and decided to go for an early dinner and shopping. Sylvia left her Par Car parked in the lot for the afternoon intending to return that evening to drive it home. However, a case of "some-timers" as she said, got the best of her and she didn't remember the golf cart until she was in her nighty and crawling into bed. The following morning, she walked to the pool to retrieve it, but it was nowhere to be found. She thought, of course, one of the more pleasant husbands, "Definitely, not grouchy Frank," Betty added, had driven it home for safety purposes and would drive it to water aerobics later in the day. No one has seen it since.

The problem with missing golf carts in the Arcadia Retirement Village stemmed from the residents; they were honest, caring citizens of an older age range. They teased each other and laughed at the golf cart mishaps, chalking them up as Sylvia had, to every Villager's favorite excuse: short term memory loss. "It's another case of 'some-timers'" was the expression most often used. However, very few in the Village were succumbing to dementia or Alzheimer's. Arcadia Retirement Villagers were generally a sharp and witty lot that simply trusted one another. It would be a hard argument to convince a Villager there could be a neighbor among them that would cause trouble or harm.

As the trio sat at Lyla's dinette table, they counted six golf carts that had come up missing in the last three weeks. Five of the six were lost under similar circumstances; one spouse left a gathering and the other stayed behind, neither paying any attention to whether the other had driven the cart home or ridden with friends. When reported, the Villagers usually requested that Officer Robertson would just "keep a lookout" as he cruised the Village. Because of their reluctance to take any missing golf carts too seriously, he always seemed reluctant to file complaints with the Chief of Police for fear the report would be published in the local newspaper. No one at the Village wanted their names printed in the Police Blotter Section on Saturdays, so most requested that Robby not file right away.

"But why would golf carts be missing?" Betty questioned. "Would someone really take them?"

"I can't imagine why," Lyla chimed in, "What can one gain from the theft of a golf cart? I could understand someone taking my jewels: they have been insured at an extremely high value and are easily hidden until sold or sent to auction, or I shudder to think, pawned. But a golf cart? How can one hide a golf cart? We must be mistaken."

The wheels in Smith's head were turning, *who would be stealing golf carts in Arcadia Retirement Village and why*? "Ladies, Lyla is probably correct. Perhaps your imaginations may be running rampant. I can't think of anyone in the Village who would deliberately take a golf cart that didn't belong to them."

"What if someone were desperate for money?" Betty asked, "Could a stolen cart provide some quick cash?"

"Maybe," Smith continued, "but not as quickly as a stolen car. Lyla's Porsche could easily be driven off down Highway 70 and hidden away in some back-alley, chop shop then sold for a hefty amount. Golf carts aren't capable of being driven extremely far on a battery and I doubt that even an amateur thief wouldn't realize a cart would be conspicuous on the highway at night. A trailer would be needed to haul them away and we haven't seen anything like that around here."

Smith had been aware of golf cart theft rings in the metropolitan area of Orlando and had seen mugshots of the perpetrators on the six o'clock evening news, but he couldn't imagine how someone could get away with an operation like that in Arcadia Retirement Village. "Most likely we're talking about 'some-timers' here, 'senior moments', rather than heists and robberies, and let's think about this seriously, who would be shifty enough to steal golf carts in the Village?"

Betty could think of a few folks that she considered untrustworthy, but she couldn't imagine them stealing golf carts. However, the rather extensive list she had bulleted on her clipboard led her to believe that something was awry in the Village. And then she remembered a rather important detail they hadn't shared with Smith, yet.

"Lyla, our trip to the antique shops!" Betty blurted, "We've forgotten to include Smith on the details of our shopping trip."

"Betty, you're absolutely right." Lyla lowered her voice for dramatic effect and turned to Smith, "We were outside the antique shops, resting under the shade of a beautiful budding magnolia just beginning to blossom on Maple Street and we heard a man's voice around the corner. He was speaking in hushed, low tones and we believed him to be on his cellphone. I was able to get a look at him, and Smith, he was clad in denim and flannel. You don't get any shiftier than denim and flannel, especially in the Florida heat. His sleeves were ripped off! They were ripped completely off! His arms were exposed, and he looked..."

"Lyla! get on with it and keep it to the essentials." Betty demanded.

"This is *all* pertinent information, Beatrice." Lyla turned back to Smith, "Getting back to the details, he was talking on his cell about taking an E Z Go. So, we got in the Porsche and followed his pickup truck. It was a dreadful sight; grey and rusty and loud; very noisy and he was speeding. Shifty in flannel and speeding, Smith."

Smith smiled at Lyla's flair for the dramatic and she continued, "Do take me seriously, Smith Kennedy."

He changed his expression to appease the actress.

"We followed this repugnant man past the Village on Highway 70 until he turned into the Low Land Palms Cattle Ranch just up the road. Beatrice took the license number, but not having paper she jotted it on her palm and it smeared. Do you remember the number at all, Beatrice?"

"Yes, yes I do. There was a G and maybe another G or an R and I remember a 9. Yes, there was definitely a 9," Betty said proudly as she bulleted those details into her notes.

"Well, that sheds new light on the idea of theft," Smith admitted. "Did you call Officer Robby?" he asked.

"Yes, we did, however, he didn't seem interested in our report," Lyla sighed. "We were a bit shaken, you understand, and slightly misled in our details that day."

"Slightly misled? How misled is slightly misled?" Smith asked.

"Misled enough to tell him that we thought a puppy had been taken illegally from someone we didn't know, by someone we didn't know, and taken somewhere but, we didn't know where." Lyla cringed remembering the conversation.

Smith furrowed his brow in disbelief, "What? After all that, you reported a missing puppy." He dropped his head into his hands.

"Smith," Lyla began, "You need not be facetious. We reported what we perceived to be the truth: a gangster clad in plaid and denim had stolen what we thought by the information we had gathered, a designer dog, which, by the way, is considerably more offensive than stealing an old golf cart! We, sir, found ourselves involved in a high-speed chase and followed him to the possible location of the aforementioned stolen property which we immediately understood to be forbidden territory to us. Believe me, we were so shaken by the events, even I began to perspire. And, when we reported our facts to Officer Robertson that day we were not yet educated on E-Z-Go Golf Carts." Lyla gasped for a breath as she finished.

Betty continued, "We are now just putting the pieces together. Don't you see it?"

Smith sat silently for a few moments. Pulling off his golf cap, he ran his fingers through his salt and pepper mop and contemplated the facts trying his best to piece it all together. It was truly a puzzle. There were several missing golf carts, but the idea of theft in the Village seemed like a far-fetched scheme presented to him by a couple of Bond-following, Hollywood elites. Still, he had to believe their story of following the sketchy fellow in flannel who whispered on his cell about a stolen E Z Go because the Kornecky's were missing an E Z Go.

"Ladies, this is quite a complex story," He began speaking carefully, choosing to use a gentle tone, "and if it is true..."

Straightening her back in a defensive gesture Betty cut Smith's sentence short, "IF? Mr. Smith? IF? I knew it, I knew it! It was a bad idea to include him, Lyla. I knew he wouldn't believe us."

Smith put both hands in the air as if to surrender. "Betty," he continued, now choosing to speak in a more commanding tone, "Betty, if this is true it is a matter for the police. I saw news coverage in Orlando about golf cart theft rings and chop shops that moved into an area, hit it hard, then got out quickly. I can hardly believe that could happen here, but just in case this is more than short-term memory loss, we should call Officer

Robertson and allow him to do any investigating that needs done. He's the one to get to the bottom of this."

Lyla and Betty both knew that Smith was right, Officer Robertson and the Arcadia Police Department would need to be called, again, and presented with this new line of thinking. There was nothing further the three of them could do concerning men in flannel, speeding pickup trucks and stolen golf carts. It was settled, Betty would call the police department and request a meeting with Officer Robby, no sirens or lights required.

Chapter 16

The following morning the Villagers woke to a cool drizzle of rain, common for early March in Florida. Lyla had spent some time on the phone with Betts telling her about the missing golf carts and the man in flannel. Although she knew she could trust her daughter, she never mentioned Smith. She had pledged her loyalty to their oath.

"Mother don't get involved. You are not James Bond and I hate to be the one to remind you, but you're just too old for this kind of nonsense." She spewed the words unapologetically. After the heart episode, Betts felt it was her responsibility to control the antics of Lyla Fontaine. The aging star had to be kept in check and apparently Auntie Beatrice was not going to do the job. "Besides, if something comes of this, you'll have the press knocking on your door. You don't want that Momma. Remember you're living as you say, *incognito*."

Before they hung up, Betts announced that she would be over for a visit at the end of the week to take her mother to lunch. They could spend the day in Punta Gorda and enjoy the quaint specialty boutiques together but no more talk about missing golf carts and pickup trucks.

Quaint - there was a word Lyla was growing tired of hearing. Everything around her was quaint: the town, the Retirement Village, even the neighbors were quiet and pleasant and *quaint*. For a time, Lyla had been quite content with quaint but now that she was rested and recovering nicely the missing golf carts were adding a new dimension to life in the Village. The excitement and mystery were exhilarating. Her mind was whirling, and her heart pumped with enthusiasm. However, she had to tread carefully in the quaint little town Arcadia. If the press were to find her, they would discover Smith Kennedy and Beatrice Brown, as well. Lyla had made an oath and a promise to her friends and wouldn't break it. Besides, she had told Betts she would remain secretly in Arcadia Retirement Village until Easter and they would worship together. But Lyla planned to tell her daughter over coffee sometime soon that shortly after the Easter celebration she would be returning to Hollywood.

As Lyla sipped her coffee, she rehearsed the lines of a poignant monologue she would deliver to Betts about returning to her home when there was a knock on the door. "Betty, what are you doing out in the chill this morning, dear? Come in. May I pour you a decaf?"

"Oh, yes, please, Lyla. That would be wonderful on this gloomy morning." Betty took the warm mug in both hands and held it tightly before she drank. "I was thinking about the conversation we're planning with Officer Robertson."

"Yes? What were you thinking?" Lyla asked.

"I don't believe it would be wise to have him come here to the Village. I think we should be cautious about who sees us in a meeting with Officer Robby. The police cruiser would draw a crowd, at least a crowd of eyes from the neighbors, if he parks in your drive or mine," Betty said thoughtfully.

"Oh, yes I agree," Lyla nodded.

Betty continued, "I think we should go to the Police Department and meet with him, discreetly, in his office. No one will see us there."

"A private meeting, Beatrice. Yes, being secretive will keep this confidential. I can be ready in thirty minutes. I'll pick you up." Lyla always insisted on driving the Porsche.

Twenty-nine minutes and thirty seconds later Lyla backed out of her drive and pulled into Betty's. "I want to commend you on the idea of remaining secretive, Beatrice. I spoke with Betts just this morning and she warned me not to get involved or allow any events to take place that may alert the press."

"That is precisely what I was concerned about Lyla. We do not want our names in the Police Blotter next Saturday. And, Lyla, we don't know who's behind this...if there is a 'this'. I'm getting a bit concerned." They chose a parking place a block from the Police Department. As they walked together Betty reminded Lyla of another important detail they could not forget, "I am Betty, and you are Anne, Anne Knight. We cannot forget that while we are here."

The two ladies arrived at noon. Officer Robertson was just coming on duty and beginning his shift in a daily meeting with other officers, so the ladies were instructed by the department assistant to wait in the lobby.

"I can't imagine the police officers' meetings are too terribly long," Betty thought out loud, "there's not a lot of action going on in Arcadia these days. Maybe when the rodeo starts up Officer Robby will have a more exciting beat than the Village." She and Lyla both smiled and nodded.

The assistant slipped behind the conference room door as the meeting was coming to a close. "Robby, you have a couple of gals from the Village wanting to see you ASAP, can I put them in your office?"

The other officers chimed in together, "A couple of girlfriends, Robby?"

"Someone's bakin' again!"

"Or some old lady lost her purse, buddy. Better get on that!"

Officer Robertson looked through the one-way mirror, "Oh no, come here and take a good look. Does the taller one look familiar?"

"Well, I'll be! That's Lyla Fontaine," exclaimed the Chief.

"I told you," said Officer Robertson. "She and the other lady, Ms. Brown are the ones that overheard Benny when he was undercover and trying to connect with Will and his boys about dumping ripped off golf carts. They are the two old gals who described him to me. I'm not sure why but they think he stole a puppy. Go figure! I don't know how they got a puppy out of that conversation, but at least they're not onto the stolen carts. But we gotta keep Lyla Fontaine low key. No press! As soon as word gets out that she's in Arcadia they'll be crawling all over town and we'll never get to the bottom of the stolen golf cart ring."

"So how do we keep her whereabouts quiet? This is Lyla Fontaine!" The Chief murmured in low tones.

"I've done some digging. She came here after a heart attack to be with her friend so she's trying to keep her whereabouts quiet, too. She's going by the name Anne Knight. I don't think we need to worry that she's trying to draw attention to herself. We just need to keep an eye out for anyone who's snooping around here looking for her, especially as the rodeo gets underway," Robby explained to them.

"But that's not all. Have you met the old guy that's fixin' up the Putt-Putt?"

One of the other officers looked hard at Robby, "Yup, sure have. He looks a lot like Smith Kennedy. What's going on there?"

"I don't know for sure; I'm working on it. I asked him for his autograph, but he told me his name was Leonard Smith. We gotta keep it all hushed though, 'til we get this golf cart thing settled." Officer Robertson turned to open the conference room door, "Now, will ya'll excuse me? I've got a Hollywood star waiting for me, boys, what's on your agenda today?" he said with a smile.

Fifteen minutes had passed when Lyla and Betty were ushered to Officer Robertson's office. His desk was tidy except for a conch shell that kept a pile of report papers from scattering when the fan oscillated in their direction.

"What can I help you young ladies with today?" Officer Robby asked with a smile.

Betty began, "Robby, I called the other day and..."

Robby interrupted, "Ms. Brown, let me assure you, I have been looking for a lost dog but haven't found any signs of dog-napping in Arcadia."

"Oh, no, no, no, Robby, we were mistaken." Betty pulled her notebook from her purse and opened it to her bullet points, "It's much worse than that. We believe that there are a number of golf carts that have been stolen in the Village and we believe that the fellow in flannel has something to do with that, not puppies but golf carts."

Officer Robertson looked intently at the two women as he listened.

Lyla continued when Betty paused for a breath, "We thought he had stolen an easy-going puppy from some loving family until the E Z Go golf carts came up missing. Do you understand Officer E-Z- Go! We are sure this fellow has some part in the thefts and Betty wrote down the license plate of the pick-up on her hand. Unfortunately, in the heat of the moment, so to speak, she developed sweaty palms and the perspiration caused most of the letters to bleed together."

"Oh true, that did happen but, I distinctly remember a G and maybe an R but there was definitely a 9 on the plate. And the truck was a rusty mess of a thing, very loud. Officer Robby, I'm sure that we could identify it. I tried to get a picture of the flannel-shirted man driving, but he was so frightening, and he scared me so badly, well, I only got a picture of the banged up front bumper as I dropped my camera. Would you like to see it?" Betty reached in her purse for her phone.

Officer Robertson's mind was racing, "Ladies, this is quite an interesting story you're telling me." He knew he had to throw them off track or the amateur detectives could foil the arrests the department had been working towards. "If you'll excuse me, I think I'll get the Chief. He may want to hear this story. Let's see what he thinks."

With the door shut behind him, Robby sprinted down the hall and around the corner. He pounded the door with the sign engraved *Chief Alfred Norton.*

"Yes?"

Robby flung the door wide open. The Chief was seated behind his desk holding his phone receiver in one hand and pushing buttons to dial with the other. "Chief, I'm sorry to barge in, but this is important."

Chief Norton put the receiver back in the cradle. "What's up, Robby? One of those gals propose to you or something?"

"You're never going to believe it," Robby began. As briefly as he could with Lyla and Betty waiting in his office, he told Chief Norton their story. "They're on to the ring and if they spook Will's boys, we may never have the chance to get 'em again."

Chief Norton leaned back in his desk chair and pursed his lips together. "Okay," he took a deep thoughtful breath, "You tell them I'm on my way down to talk to them. I'll put an end to this right here and now. We don't need a couple of senior citizens from the Retirement Village messing this up for us. You're the good cop already, so I'm going to be the bad cop. Now what are their names? I'm gonna scare them so bad they'll hide behind that stucco wall and never come out!"

Officer Robertson returned to his office and found the ladies talking in low tones about the man in the flannel shirt. They were preparing to give the Chief a complete description and did not want to miss a single detail. Chief Norton followed shortly after Robby with a manilla file in his hand. The corner was flagged with an orange tag and he tossed it on the desk so the ladies could plainly see their names, ANNE KNIGHT & BETTY BROWN: ARCADIA RETIREMENT VILLAGE, scrawled across the top.

"Good morning or excuse me, I guess it's afternoon now isn't it, ladies? It seems that we all make mistakes every now and then, don't we?" Chief Norton smiled at them both.

Lyla and Betty nodded, and Chief Norton's amiable countenance transformed. His eyes glared at the women and his voice lowered to a growl. He turned his back to them and began slowly, "Officer Robertson has told me about your little adventure." He paused and turned back to face them, "It seems that you've made a rather dangerous mistake, ladies. You took it upon yourselves to become a couple of amateur detectives. That is a mistake I do not want to hear about again. Do not, and I repeat DO NOT eavesdrop on conversations, follow anyone in your car or even worry your pretty little heads about crime in Arcadia. Crime fighting is a job for my officers, definitely not for a couple of ladies your," he paused again and chose his words carefully, "well, of your capacity, we'll say."

Lyla whisked her long grey curls back over her shoulder and shot him a disapproving scowl. She opened her mouth to speak.

The Chief moved toward her, leaned down and put a hand on each arm of the chair she was sitting in. She pushed herself back into the chair as far as she could. Looking directly at her, eye-to-eye, Chief Norton growled, "Don't make the mistake of looking for trouble and don't start spreading gossip about Arcadia. We don't want bad press, do we lady? Got it ma'am?"

With that, Chief Norton stood, looking much taller than he did when he entered, turned on his heel and left the room. Officer Robinson offered Lyla and Betty advice, "Don't cross the boss, ladies. Don't let your imaginations run away with you. This is Arcadia, for goodness sake." Officer Robertson turned his eyes to Lyla, "Nothing happens here, isn't that why you moved here, ma'am? Now, shall I walk you to your car?"

"No thank you, sir, we are quite capable, even in our... capacity." Lyla replied defiantly. Officer Robertson opened the office door.

Getting the last word, Lyla huffed, "Let's go, Betty."

Chapter 17

"Johnson, hey, Johnson!" Smith yelled from the office window, "Check the windmill, it seemed to jerk a bit as it turned yesterday. Let me know if I need to have the installers look it over. They're coming in tomorrow for a final check before the grand opening next weekend."

Johnson began to slowly walk the eighteen holes, carefully checking the angles of the putts and the length from tee to cup and flag. After returning from Ireland, the Putt-Putt didn't excite him, however his father's recovery did. Sitting at his father's bedside in Florida Hospital in Orlando three months earlier, Johnson had worried that Smith's cognizance wouldn't fully return and the two would never experience the fullness of the relationship they had grown to appreciate.

In the stark ICU room, he had held his father's hand and prayed for strength, confessing that he was not ready to parent his parent. As Johnson drifted in and out of his prayers, his mind wandered back to his childhood. He vaguely remembered an elderly pastor in a suit and tie preaching from a pulpit positioned in front of a stained-glass picture of Jesus. The enormous Jesus held a lamb in his arms as he glistened in the morning sun pouring into the sanctuary.

He pictured himself sitting in the pew next to his father and mother. Johnson grew up hearing the sermons instructing him to obey the *Big 10*, as his father called the commandments. As a teen, he would huff at the word obey and found little enjoyment obeying his earthly father's command to attend church on Sunday mornings, forgoing golf outings with his buddies. He remembered whispering to God as his father pounded on his bedroom door every week rousing him in time for the 10:00 a.m. service, "If I don't have to go to church this weekend, God, I promise I'll go next weekend. I'll even try to obey the Big 10."

Although he never really meant to keep the oath as a teen, sitting next to his father during the dark moments in the hospital ICU Johnson found himself bargaining with God more seriously. He laid out a mental contract with Him, "Lord, if you restore my dad's mind and body, I promise, I'll definitely go back to church." He pledged the oath, and this time he meant it, unfortunately he just hadn't found the time to keep it, yet.

While walking the Putt-Putt course Johnson tried to find a loophole in this deal he'd cut with the Almighty and he wandered onto hole 15. Smith had followed the cement sidewalk along the course edge until he found his son shaking his head as he scrutinized what Crystal claimed to be the hole that would bring in the customers, the giant hippo. Johnson suddenly felt much like a motorist on the highway viewing a bad accident; not that the passers-by want to see the effects of the mangled car, it just becomes almost humanly impossible to look away. He felt the same about the hippo. He couldn't decide if he was fascinated or appalled by the mechanical animal as it opened and shut its mouth snatching golf balls into the abyss of the hippo's digestive tract before depositing them out the other end in the direction of the cup.

"Don't say a word, Johnson, don't say a word." Smith could read the inner workings of the younger golfer's mind. "Your mother used to advise me to invest in Putt-Putt. She would tell me it was an investment in families and first dates. Am I right?"

Johnson lifted his shoulders and dropped them with an acquiescing sigh.

"So, this is in her honor. Don't say a word!" the elder said to end any patronizing comments.

Johnson knew the reverence his father held for his mother so just as he was taught as a teenager years earlier, he obeyed. He did as Smith said and kept his opinions to himself although he found it difficult to honor his mother with a golf ball-eating hippopotamus.

Dropping the subject, he turned the conversation to quizzing his dad on health issues. "What did the doctor say on your last visit?"

"I'm as fit as a fiddle and released from my physical therapist," Smith informed his son with a smile. "He's given me a great routine of exercises to follow but I'm still working on my drive. I can't seem to get past the slice in my swing."

"So, what's new with that, Dad? Sounds like the old Smith Kennedy if you ask me," Johnson smirked. "Does that mean you'll be heading home?"

"Hey! Watch it, boy!" Smith landed a father-son punch on Johnson's bicep and laughed. "Once I get the Putt-Putt up and going, and into the capable hands of Crystal Bell, I think I will. I'll be close enough that I can drive over every week for a day to keep the maintenance up and the schedule in order." Smith paused to contemplate his next thought before sharing it with his son, "Honestly, though, I'm not in a big rush. I feel rather good about what I've accomplished here but we both know it's small potatoes compared to the courses we've designed together."

Johnson could hear the apprehension ringing in his father's voice, "Dad, we've always designed together, we can continue to work on layouts and..."

"I'm not so sure I'm ready to tackle anything that major," Smith interjected, "I've been thinking about starting something new. I've got a lot of knowledge and know-how stored up here," Smith tapped the side of his head with his pointer finger. "I'd like to share it, maybe write a few golf instruction guides or better yet, make golf videos. Who wouldn't want to learn from a master, am I right?"

Johnson knew there was no argument against that idea. He nodded his head in agreement.

"But don't think you'll get rid of me too easily, son," Smith quipped. "I pledge to be your resident consultant, on call any time, willing to travel and give my stamp of approval on any course layout you design!"

Johnson laughed and threw his arm around his dad's shoulder as they made their way to the end of the course. The duo looked up from the 18th hole and Johnson spotted a silver Porsche parked next to the Highlander. "Nice car! Maybe Putt-Putt golf isn't so bad after all." Lyla stood at the driver's side door and waved at Smith. Johnson elbowed his father, "And, it seems to attract interesting clientele."

Smith led the way to the Porsche reminding himself with each step to introduce Lyla as Anne. "Ms. Knight, I'd like you to meet my son, Johnson. Johnson, this is Anne Knight, a friend of mine."

Lyla pulled her locks back with her sunglasses and smiled, lips held shut to hide the gap between her front teeth. "How do you do, Johnson. It's a pleasure to meet you, dear. That must be your car I've parked next to; I saw it at your father's cottage this morning. We're neighbors, Leonard and I."

"It's nice to meet you, Ms. Knight. Great Porsche, mind if I take a look?"

"Not at all. I just stopped to say hello to your father. May I borrow him for a moment?" Lyla walked to the two men and slid her arm in Smith's. "May we speak in the office, Leonard?

Johnson shot a sideways glance at his father. It was one of those looks his father had given him when he announced he'd asked Julia Benoit to the prom back in high school. "He's all yours," he said with a fatherly tone.

Johnson circled the car, noting Lyla and Smith's whispering as they stepped inside the office doorway. "Smith, it happened again, another cart is missing. Phil and Lois Wilcox left it at the Club House last night and walked home together. This time when they called Officer Robertson they were sure where they left it."

"No 'some-timers'?" Smith questioned.

"No," Lyla assured him, "they are dead sure they left it to walk home and enjoy the stars. It was a clear night and Phil was picking out the constellations, a hobby he enjoys. When he walked back to retrieve it this morning, it was gone! And there's more to the story according to Blanche and her grapevine posse."

Smith laughed out loud, "Since when have you become a recipient of grapevine gossip?"

"I made up my mind a few days ago to have coffee in the Club House in the mornings. It's an undercover assignment I gave myself to retrieve information, Smith, valuable information. So, while on assignment this morning, I learned that Phil and Lois called Officer Robby requesting that he file a report and Robby has been rather reticent to do so." Lyla squinted and furrowed her brow, "Call it woman's intuition but something is amiss. I plan to get to the bottom of it before I move back home to Beverly Hills. There's trouble brewing in paradise, sir."

Smith nodded in agreement, "So, what will your next assignment be, 'Ms. Bond'?"

"Well, I'm glad you asked." Lyla lifted her chin in confidence and continued, "I need you and Betty to help me, please. I'd like to strategize ASAP. Will you be spending the entire day with your son?"

"He'll be here the rest of the day but driving back to Naples this evening." Smith had become intrigued with Lyla's observations, "How about eight o'clock tonight?" he offered.

"That will work fine for me. I'll get ahold of Betty." Lyla walked back to her Porsche and stood beside Johnson. "She's a beauty, isn't she?"

"Yes, she certainly is," Johnson said as he patted the hood and looked up to meet Lyla's eyes. "Boy, you look a lot like that actress, Lyla Fontaine."

"Why thank you for the compliment, dear, I get that occasionally, although I really don't see the resemblance." Lyla looked back at the office to see Smith still standing in the doorway, "See you tonight, Leonard, eight o'clock."

Johnson bounded up the steps and into the office, "So you have a date? I didn't know Arcadia was home to Porsche-driving babes your age, Dad. No wonder you're not in a rush to head back to Orlando."

Chapter 18

Betty arrived at Lyla's an hour early. "What's going on? What do you have cooking up in that scheming, little, brain of yours?" Betty questioned Lyla with little effect. She mysteriously refused to reveal her plan until Smith arrived.

"My goodness, Lyla, do we really need," Betty left a dramatic pause to solidify her point, "Smith?" She rolled her eyes to drive home the point, "He's all wrapped up in that golf course of his. Besides, you and I have taken on the world in the past, Lyla. We can do it again, just the two of us."

Lyla kept Betty at bay, "You're absolutely right about the past but, it's a new day and we need him to effectively work this plan, dear. I'll explain it all when he arrives, until then, you're wasting your breath, I'm not divulging anything."

A few minutes before eight the Highlander pulled into Smith's drive. On their way in from Highway 70 the two men chuckled as they drove past Venus De Milo now decked out in a cowboy hat with a bandana neatly tied around her neck. "According to Venus, it's almost rodeo time in Arcadia. They say it's a big deal here." Smith declared.

In the driveway, Smith climbed out of the passenger's door and walked to the driver's side to shake his son's hand before Johnson left the Village. "Good to see you, Dad. I'm relieved your recovery has gone so well. You know, I was afraid you were completely nuts when you wanted to buy the Putt-Putt and now look at you, getting ready to invest in families and first dates! And on top of that, I had to have you home in time for a rendezvous of your own!"

Smith patted Johnson's arm, "Slow down, Trigger! Ms. Knight is just a friend. I'll call you in a few days, drive safely." He breathed a prayer of thanksgiving for such a caring son.

With his father deposited safely at the ocean blue cottage, Johnson waved to the two women on the front porch of the pink cottage across the street. Betty and Lyla were wrapped in sweaters in the cool evening breeze. Smith strode over to them with golf club in hand as Ellwood McCoy watched silently from under his carport.

The three took their places at the dinette table in the breakfast nook. Lyla set out three etched, lead glass tumblers and retrieved a matching pitcher of lemonade from the refrigerator. She made the drink from a package mix but when she added fresh lemon slices and ice, she felt compelled to silently congratulate herself on how delightful it looked. The sight of the cheery nook adorned with friends seated at her table roused Lyla's excitement of returning to Beverly Hills and reviving her role as hostess to dinner parties and art galas once again.

For a brief moment, Lyla drifted back to her mansion making a mental guest list for her first post-heart attack gathering. Inviting Smith Kennedy would be a must. Their friendship had struck a harmonious chord and he was proving to be a rather pleasant companion. Even though he had made a living hitting a little ball around who knows where, it served him well and despite his interest in the sports world, she had grown to appreciate his thoughtfulness. She didn't want to lose the connection with him.

Beatrice would be invited as well, of course. As Lyla's best friend and confidant, she would be asked to stay for an extended holiday. Lyla hoped maybe Beatrice would enjoy life back in the clamor of Hollywood again and, maybe she could be persuaded to move back home.

Jacque Louis would cater the event and lemonade made from freshly squeezed lemons, not a powder mix, would be served. Maybe lemonade would become her signature drink...

"Lyla," Betty's voice interrupted her daydream, "Dear, are you ever going to tell us why we're here?"

Lyla jerked back to the present, "Of course, Beatrice. We need to focus our attention on Arcadia Retirement Village and missing golf carts. I've been thinking and I believe there is more happening here than meets the eye. Somebody is taking advantage of the good people of the Village and we need to get to the bottom of this! We need to crack this caper."

Betty laughed out loud, "Isn't that what you told James Bond in *The Madrid Caper*?"

"Well, yes, it is!" Lyla proclaimed, "But it certainly fits this moment as well, don't you agree?"

Smith set his glass of lemonade on the table, "Okay Ladies, if you're going to hook me into a 'caper' of sorts, you're going to have to tell me what it is, and what my role will be in the script."

"It's hard to say, Smith," Betty confessed. "When Lyla is directing you just don't know what you're getting into. Get ready!"

Lyla paused and carefully chose her words, "I have to begin by begging you both to hear me out, without interruption or dispute."

Smith and Betty winced in tandem, "It's that kind of 'caper'?" Smith asked, "What are you proposing here, Lyla?"

"Well, Smith, you've really hit the nail on the head with that phrase because I am proposing a proposal, of sorts." Lyla watched the wince on the faces of her companions turn to bewilderment. "We've frequently discussed the missing golf carts and the peculiar occurrences in each situation. Betty has these bulleted nicely in her notebook so no need to rehash them, but I have been thinking," Lyla paused again dramatically sucking in a deep breath before continuing. "We could plan a sting, a set-up! We would photograph the crooks and identify them for the police."

Betty immediately protested, "Lyla, I disapprove already! We were strictly forbidden to get involved by Chief Norton. We could end up on the six o'clock news and that would be the end of my quiet retirement here in the Village. I can see the lights, sirens, reporters and Six O'clock Action News camped on your doorstep to get the latest on the great Lyla Fontaine now in cahoots with Smith Kennedy, golfer extraordinaire!"

"Now, Beatrice, you promised not to interrupt. You must allow me to finish."

In her earlier years, Lyla found great enjoyment in her Hollywood star power, announcing her demands causing those around her to jump into action. She had often manipulated her friend, Beatrice, into doing her bidding. However, the heart attack altered her thinking and began to pull on her heart strings ever so slightly.

Sitting quietly in her little pink cottage, thankful that God had seen fit to give her an encore, a second act in which to live, she reviewed her success. It became evident that she had lived a rather shallow existence through movie credits and talk show conversations. During an honest, hard look in the mirror, while pulling the skin at her temples back to her hairline with her pointer finger and tightening her sagging chin with her thumb, she realized her Hollywood friends had been friends because of her influence and money. All except Beatrice, the only one who had stood by her from the beginning.

With this newfound insight, Lyla made the decision that during her encore provided by God she would treasure this friendship with Beatrice and not take it for granted. Although she had to admit to herself, it would not be easy, it was time to put Beatrice's wishes above her own. She would allow Beatrice to be "Betty" which also meant she would take on the responsibility to not disrupt Betty's life of Canasta card parties and bus trips.

But a conflict was brewing in Lyla. While she desperately wanted to care for and love her friend, she was compelled to do something on behalf of the residents of the Village. Something bigger than herself, something grander than Betty's anonymity, something that she could only determine to be her inner James Bond was stirring her to action.

Moving into the pink cottage had set the stage for Lyla's comeback giving her time to rest and restore, body, mind, and soul. Fantasies of thugs stealing her jewels became distant and less frequent. Lately, she lay quietly in bed in the early morning hours, remembering the few sermons she had heard Betts preach. She contemplated the thought that God loved her and as Betts had said, wanted her to love him, in return. God had a plan and though it was confusing, evidently for Lyla, it included a heart attack followed by recovery played out in a hidden retirement village where few knew her.

Before the heart attack Lyla had a propensity to pray only occasionally, on sleepless nights in times of trouble, but lately she found herself praying prayers of thankfulness at all hours of the day. She was shocked when out of the blue she thanked God for a regular heartbeat, and lungs that drew in breath, two things she had always taken for granted. She noticed the sunset and the beauty of the world around her and wondered why she hadn't taken notice of it all before. Her prayers were filled with spoken words of thanksgiving for this God that loved her as Lyla Fontaine but more intimately as Anne Knight. And she was especially thankful for a daughter that had made her aware of His love. She was grateful for her two dear friends, Betty and Smith. Lyla surprised herself by asking God to care for them, not just requesting a list of things for herself. She was learning to view life from a new perspective that caused the fear of aging to diminish and the excitement of what was yet to come began to grow in her soul. Betts had whispered to her in her hospital room, "God has plans for you mother, plans with a future and there's hope in that, hope that He will restore you and use you to bless others."

Sitting at the table with her friends, sharing lemonade lifted Lyla's spirit to a philosophical notion, "Betty, Smith, I don't think we should worry so about taking a risk every now and then. We spent our younger days taking risks. Smith won the Masters because he took a risk and became competitive in the game of golf. I took a risk and signed my name to a contract with a talent agent back in Swartz Creek. Beatrice, your career revolved around the success of others and you took a risk signing on with me. So why stop now, we'll be like the stars!"

Smith wondered out loud, "What stars are you talking about, Lyla?"

"The stars in the heavens, Smith." Lyla exclaimed, "I've been reading lately, about the stars. Did you know that a star burns brighter as it grows older and is brightest just before it dies? This is our chance to blaze!"

Betty jumped from her chair and flung her arms around her friend, "Lyla! Are you dying? Oh, Lyla!" Betty began to sob, "Whatever will I do without you? How much time do you have left, dear?"

For a split second, Lyla Fontaine considered returning to her old ways and whispering a little lie *"Yes, Beatrice and to have you help me is my dying wish..."* to coerce Betty into her plan, but instead, Lyla drew strength and pushed that thought from her mind. "No, no dear, I'm not dying, not anytime soon, that is," she said between Betty's sobs.

"Then what is this all about? You're talking nonsense; blazing stars and our chance to burn out?" Betty sniffled and wiped her nose with a tissue.

"Our chance to blaze, Beatrice! Let's blaze and not burn out," corrected Lyla.

Smith jumped in, "That was inspiring, I think, but I'm lost here, maybe you should begin again, Lyla, and get to the point of this meeting."

Lyla dropped her palms on the table, "Listen, we have a chance to do something extraordinary for the Village. Before I leave here, I want to make a difference as *Anne Knight*. I think the three of us can put an end to the missing golf carts. I have a thought about how to corner the crooks and I've formulated a magnificent plan. That is our chance to blaze! We'll burn brighter than we ever have by helping the people around us. Can you understand that?"

"Capisce!" exclaimed Smith, "That, my dear, was straight forward. Now, what is this plan you've concocted?"

"Okay, now hold onto your hats because it's an exceptional plan but it needs all of our cooperation. You two, Leonard Smith and Betty Brown, need to become the newest couple in the Arcadia Retirement Village," Lyla said with glee.

"Not on your life!" Betty proffered as she stood to her feet, "That is the most ridiculous plan I've ever heard! I would never be a couple with this man and why would you suggest such a thing, Lyla?"

Smith pushed back his chair and stood defensively across the table, "And why is that? Why would you 'never be a couple with *this* man'? What makes you and your dandelion-plucker think you could do better? You never did like me, did you, Betty Brown?"

With her sentimentality totally unnerved, Lyla shouted, "This is what I asked you not to do!" She threw her hands into the air above her head, "Do not interrupt or dispute until I am entirely finished, do you understand?"

Both Smith and Betty took their seats again. "What are we getting into?" Betty whimpered.

"Listen to the plan, you two, consider it to just be a script, much like a movie script, with parts for the actors to play. You two will simply act out the parts. It's simple and you can do this." Lyla explained, "You are both exciting, attractive people and the Village will delight seeing you together. I've done my research. I've been having coffee in the Club House every morning chatting it up. This will lure Blanche right into the plan and the gossip will travel the grapevine in a flash!"

Lyla laid out her plan, "As a new couple you'll be seen together throughout the Village: a gala at the Club House, sitting in the sun at the pool, riding through the Village with the wind romantically blowing through your hair in that expensive Club Car. And, for the pièce de résistance you must be together at the grand opening of the little golf course you've been remodeling, Smith."

"Well, we had planned to ask you if you needed our help," interjected Betty. "We were going to come, anyway."

"Really? That's truly thoughtful of the both of you, but I'm restoring the place to its former glory *not* remodeling or redecorating it like you would a bathroom," Smith sighed. "But what does this have to do with missing golf carts, Lyla?"

"At just the right moment we'll leave that little beauty you drive out in the open with the keys in the ignition and watch and wait! It will practically be screaming for a thug to swoop in and grab it." Lyla's voice grew with excitement. "We'll hide and wait for someone to take it and get a picture of the perpetrator in the get-away vehicle. I'm sure it will match the description of the old grey truck. We'll have all the information we need to immediately call 911. We'll catch the thief, red handed and let the Arcadia Police Department get the credit! Chief Norton and Officer Robertson will revel in that victory! It's a simple plan and it can't go wrong."

"I don't know, Lyla," Smith said slowly. "I don't know if using my Club Car is such a good idea. Plus, I'm not sure Betty and I can act, well, you know, like a couple? I'm just not sure we could ever pull that off."

Lyla pushed her chair back from the table and stood to command their attention, "Smith, do you remember our first conversation? We discussed the fact that we have not found ourselves here in the Arcadia Retirement Village serendipitously. It's hardly probable that two recuperating stars, whether on the screen or on the golf course, would find themselves in the same retirement village, off the beaten path at the same time unless, well, unless it was the result of some grand design."

Smith tapped the end of the golf club on the floor as he contemplated the idea, "Lyla Fontaine, I believe you may be right. For the two of us, no, all three of us to find ourselves here at such a time as this in our lives, we must relinquish to the Designer."

"Oh! My word!" Betty interrupted, "this is outlandish! We are three *mature* adults; can we please think as such? Or do I need to remind you that as geriatrics we are much too old to be chasing crooks and blazing like stars. Lyla, I settled in Arcadia Retirement Village to retire. I would like to burn out quietly! Simply to enjoy a peaceful life, so let's just put aside any notion of crime fighting and quietly enjoy."

Smith countered, "Yes, Betty, but the peaceful lives of the Arcadia Retirement Village will be forced to walk to the Piggly Wiggly if someone doesn't get to the bottom of this mess. I say we join Lyla by 'cracking this caper' James Bond style." Lyla's appeal had sparked a blaze within Smith. "I may be old but I'm not dead, yet! So, I'm all in Lyla, let's blaze! We'll end this Village crime spree!"

Lyla smiled her signature smile revealing the space between her two front teeth. She had an ally in Smith.

"Come on Ms. Brown be my girlfriend," Smith smiled as he playfully removed his golf cap and lay it across his heart. "Except my proposal and play the part with me!"

Betty shook her head, "I am far too old to play the role of a girlfriend."

Lyla stood dramatically poised with her back straight and jaw jutted forward in confidence. She began slowly gaining rhythm as she spoke, "Betty Brown, I '*will not go gentle into that good night, Old age should burn and rave at close of day; Rage, rage against the dying of the light.'"*[1] Lyla continued rebelling against her past attitudes of age, "I am not 'over the hill', I do not have one foot in the grave. I am alive and it's time to live."

Both Betty and Smith, spellbound, were unable to look away. They were mesmerized by her conviction.

Lyla sat down at the table and lifted her lemonade, "Are you with me?"

She was surprised by the intensity that compelled her to rescue the good residents of the Village. If the Arcadia Police Department wouldn't do it, she would! "We just need to get that Club Car left at the Club House, seemingly by accident, and then we'll call the police when it's heisted. That's all we need to do," Lyla promised.

She reached across the dinette table and took Betty by the hand, "Beatrice, you've lived your life behind the camera, but you have always had an eye for talent and a flair for the dramatic. I'm sure you can play the part of the star-crossed lover so persuasively that when you leave Smith's Club Car unattended everyone will believe you did so because you were blinded by love. The crooks will jump at the chance to take it. Will you do it, dear?"

---

1 *The Poems of Dylan Thomas*, published by New Directions. Copyright © 1952, 1953 Dylan Thomas. Copyright © 1937, 1945, 1955, 1962, 1966, 1967 the Trustees for the Copyrights of Dylan Thomas. Copyright © 1938, 1939, 1943, 1946, 1971 New Directions Publishing Corp.

Silence fell in the cottage. Lyla and Smith eagerly waited for Betty's response. Betty could hear her heart pounding in her chest as she woefully considered their plan. Her left-brain feared this 'caper' as her friends called it, may go awry at any moment but in her right-brain an excitement stirred. She couldn't help but imagine what it would be like to revel in the glory of a team of victorious crime busters. "I don't see how we can ever pull this off and if it all goes south and I have to move from here to save face, I'll never forgive either of you," Betty scowled, "but I'll do it."

Lyla wanted to let out a "Whoop!" but instead kept her composure, "We've taken on the world many times Betty, just the two of us, but now we have a comrade in arms. With Smith on our side, we'll blaze! How can we go wrong?"

"Smith? We'll see about that." Betty grumbled. Smith Kennedy was the very reason she was worried she could never play her part convincingly.

Chapter 19

Thursday Night Canasta Club became the target of Smith and Betty's grand reveal as a couple. The prospect of Blanche Thomson being planted in her favorite armchair in the corner of the Club House was promising. Thriving on Village gossip she fed off the manna of the many Club House gatherings and the trio was confident Blanche would be the perfect catalyst to propagate the news of the coupling of Leonard Smith and Betty Brown throughout the Village. The plan was discussed, and once again, Betty wrote it out in bullet points for the two to study and carefully follow.

- Smith – pick up Betty & ride together in Club Car
- Smith – Walk to Club House with his arm around Betty
- Smith – acknowledge Blanche to draw her attention

- Play as partners – (Smith learn how to play game before that night)
- Laugh and smile across table
- Hold hands while leaving
- Betty – suggest they walk home
- Smith – remind Betty they have golf cart

It looked fairly elementary on paper but as Smith analyzed the bullet points, he began to realize the depth of his role as the pursuer. Dating Claire had been easy and natural. They fit together from the very beginning and she fully captured his attention. After she was gone, he had little interest in other women. He just couldn't muster the energy for planning an evening of small talk and all the nerves and angst that went with it, so this role would truly be a grand performance. He wondered if he could be believable and appear as if he sincerely had an interest in the dandelion-plucker wielding Betty Brown?

As Betty wrote out the details in her notebook, he studied her from across the table. He couldn't think of a single time they had spoken alone; she had always been accompanied by Lyla Fontaine (except for the unfortunate incident in the front yard). Lyla's unassailable charisma had paled Betty but now that he looked at her intently as the character of his girlfriend, he was surprised; she was an attractive woman. She was naturally pretty without much makeup except for a little color on her cheeks and lips. She was genuinely kind, except to him, of course, but he believed that to be her protective instinct for Lyla. She was somewhat reticent to adventure, so he felt a respect for her willingness to be a member of the crime fighting team they had formed.

Betty looked up from her bullet points and caught Smith's eye, "You know, Smith, I think we can do this. We may be able to pull this off." She smiled at him and Smith began to think he might be able to play the part quite believably.

It was decided that Lyla would not attend the coming-out of Leonard and Betty. Her morning coffees were the only Club House tête-à-têtes in which she had shown interest. Having not attended a single card party yet, making a grand entrance now would appear somewhat suspicious. The couple certainly did not want to give the appearance they needed a chaperone, either. Although Lyla was greatly disappointed, she agreed it might be questionable if she came along, but Smith and Betty agreed to meet at her cottage following the card game to give her the rundown of the evening.

Thursday came quickly. That afternoon Betty instructed Smith during a crash course in Canasta as they prepared for the evening. Smith's competitive nature made him a quick student to the game, but Betty was sure he would be no match for the cutthroats playing around their table. "We won't worry about winning," she consoled him, "we just need to be believable."

After Smith's tutoring session, Lyla helped Betty choose an attractive outfit to wear for the evening. Betty dressed in white capris and a button down, lavender, cap sleeve blouse. She pulled the collar up around the back of her neck where it met her neatly cut, auburn died bob. Lyla brought her an oversized, multi-colored beaded necklace from her collection that lay beautifully against the lavender blouse. At the last minute, Betty slipped into her Neiman Marcus sandals that squeezed her feet and threw a multi-colored straw bag over her shoulder that matched the necklace. She looked stunning.

Betty laughed as she looked in the mirror. "Lyla, dear, I feel like I'm off to the prom! I'm just sporting a few more wrinkles than I did back then. And just look at my ankles, oh goodness, when did my knees drop down there?"

They laughed out loud and Lyla snapped a picture. "I could write a screenplay about this, Beatrice. Who shall I get to play you?"

"I know just the person," Betty laughed, "Could you pull a few strings and get Lyla Fontaine?"

"I hardly think so, haven't you heard the news? She's been missing for weeks. I heard she moved to a quaint little Village in Florida and no one has seen her since!"

Lyla walked across the street to her cottage before Smith climbed in the Club Car and swung by to pick up Betty. She watched from the window as he left his golf club in the cart and walked to her door to properly retrieve her as a gentleman. The two smiled and looked quite comfortable with each other as they sat side-by-side in the Club Car whirring down Sunset Lane to the Club House. Lyla could hardly contain her curiosity as she waited for their return later that evening. She laughed as she considered walking up to the Club House and pressing her nose against the window to peer inside. Lemonade in hand, she sat on the front porch and tried reading to pass the time, but her mind merely wandered through the words. She finally turned on a cable cooking channel, poured herself a second glass of cold lemonade and began to plan the menu for her first big gala on her return to Beverly Hills.

Smith strategically parked the Club Car on the far side of the parking lot providing the two ample distance to walk past the resident mailboxes that were mounted under an awning outside of the Club House. As they strolled together, Smith placed his hand on the small of Betty's back and the buzz began. She leaned in close to him and whispered, "I feel like I'm back in

Hollywood walking the Red Carpet, but honestly, that wasn't nearly as nerve racking as this!"

He kept his hand in position on Betty's back as they approached the Club House entryway. The glass wall provided a clear view for all players at the canasta tables to see the two laughing and talking as Smith reached for the door to pull it open for Betty. All eyes were on them and all mouths were jaw-dropped.

"Remember, tonight you have to call me Leonard," Smith reassured as his hand urged her through the door and she took the first step into the building. Betty had completely forgotten that Smith was Leonard or Leonard was Smith, whatever the moment called for!

She quietly replied, "Thank you, Leonard," to plant the name in her mind for the evening.

Smith allowed the door to close lightly behind them, "Here we go."

The room fell silent momentarily. Blanche Thompson looked up from her newspaper and Smith nodded in her direction. She immediately reached for the cell phone in her purse.

George and Connie, Betty's Canasta table partners for the evening were the first to respond. "Hey! Over here Betty. Glad to see you brought a friend." George offered an extra chair.

"George and Connie, I'd like to introduce you to a new friend of mine, Leonard Smith. We met the night of the new neighbor party."

"Well, buddy, we're glad you're here," George said as he gave Smith a pat on the back.

David Willoughby pulled a chair alongside Smith before the game began, "Tell me about that wicked classy Club Car you're driving, Ace. She's a beauty, she is." Smith proudly proclaimed the grandeur of the cart, even embellishing a bit to David on all the extras he'd added. He was in hopes that the information would be overheard and passed along to the ear of some interested thief.

Punch and coffee were available on a table near the wall. After David returned to his table, Smith put his arm on the back of Betty's chair and asked loudly enough for Blanche to hear, "Can I get you a cup of coffee, Bette?"

"Sure Len," Betty replied and smiled, holding back a giggle. She was actually enjoying the role of Leonard Smith's love interest. Acting the part was far easier than she had expected, and the evening was playing out better than she ever imagined it would.

Only three hands had been played when a couple members of Blanche's posse strolled in making the excuse that they needed some decaf. The ladies gathered in the corner around Blanche and talked quietly with eyes darting in the direction of Betty and Smith's table.

Many of the card players had questions about the Putt-Putt grand opening and accolades were given to Smith for the excellent work that had been accomplished. It was what many concluded to be an enhancement to the local community of Arcadia and a welcoming sight as vacationers drove up and down Highway 70.

George poured himself a glass of punch and began to reminisce to the room that his first date with Connie was at a Putt-Putt. "Connie was so sweet back then. She let me put my arms around her to help her with her golf swing. Whew, made me weak in the knees, it did!"

George sighed but Connie set him straight, "George Sawyer! The only time you and I have ever played Putt-Putt was with our grandchildren. I don't know who that first date was with, but it wasn't me!" The other players chuckled as she put her cards face down on the table and threw her arms in the air, "Weak in the knees? I'd like to know who made you weak in the knees because it definitely wasn't me."

"It wasn't you, Connie? That must be why I remember the gal being so sweet," George said with a wink and a snicker to the others around the table. He shouted across the room to David Willoughby, "Hey, Dave, you got a couch I can sleep on, buddy? Looks like I may need it tonight!"

The evening unfolded as planned. Leonard even proved to be somewhat competitive in Canasta and as the night ended, Betty left the table feeling far less embarrassed than she had anticipated. The new couple prepared to leave, and Betty recited her rehearsed line convincingly, "This was such a nice evening I'm glad we'll end it with a walk home."

Smith laughed quite naturally and off his tongue rolled, "Betty, you must have forgotten, we brought the Club Car, we'll walk another time."

Betty pretended to be embarrassed answering with a prepared "Oh, that's right," as they waved goodbye to the room. Reaching the Club Car Betty dropped into her seat, "Mission accomplished, Leonard!"

"Betty Brown, you missed your calling, your name should have blazed in lights. You were so convincing that I believed you myself." They laughed side-by-side in the Club Car on the way to Lyla's and shouted "hello" when they noticed Ellwood sitting in the dark on his front porch.

Chapter 20

Crystal Bell flung wide the door to the Putt-Putt office and shouted "Three days, boss! And it sure looks like we are ready to roll. Can you believe it? We have golf balls in every color of the rainbow and large, medium and small putters ready to slide into the rack. The score sheets are printed, the food trucks are coming, the staff is trained! Holy cats, we are set except for one thing."

"I bet I know what you think we're missing." Smith pointed to the window, "Look out there, young lady."

Crystal ran to the window and gasped. There it was, a lime green, LED sign with bold, black lettering leaning against the Putt-Putt course wall. She read, "Claire's Putt-Putt Golf Course" aloud to Smith. "It's a beauty, boss. You know that wife of yours is lookin' down here on ya and she's awfully proud of ya!" Crystal blinked back a misty tear. "I just know she is."

Smith didn't have words to respond. He simply smiled at Crystal's compassion and her childlike theology.

"When's it going up?" she questioned.

"Don't you worry about that; the crew will have it mounted on the pole out at the highway before the opening," Smith assured.

The To-Do list Smith had kept for months had dwindled to a few final items that he would complete in the next few days. This allowed him plenty of time to be seen in the Village with Betty. He shot her a text: *Pick u up at 3 for pool.* A few seconds later his phone buzzed announcing a return text and a thumbs up emoji appeared on his screen.

Betts had called her mother inquiring if Lyla would be available for coffee that morning. She would stop on her way to a state-wide meeting and assembly of pastors in Fort Myers. Lyla had decided she couldn't bear to miss a moment of action. After coffee with her daughter, she would head to the pool arriving before the happy new couple and sit in a chaise lounge with a glass of lemonade. Lyla put on her swimming suit and pulled a beach cover-up over top.

As Betts pulled in the drive, Lyla set a colorful pitcher of lemonade on the table with the etched, led-glass tumblers hoping her daughter would take notice. "Hello, my beautiful daughter," Lyla called out from the kitchen as Betts opened the screen.

"Mother? Is that you? Am I in the right cottage?" Betts had taken note of her mother's change of character lately and immediately regretted her teasing, waiting for Lyla to respond by mapping out a guilt trip with no exit.

"Oh, Betts, can't a mother dote on her only daughter?" Lyla quipped back.

Betts bit her tongue in shock at Lyla's sweetness. She had never raised her voice as a mother, nor spoken vulgar words to Betts, but she had often thrown words like stones and built a barricade between them. A wall that served little purpose, much like the four foot of stucco that ran across the front of the Village. But Lyla's heart attack had softened her and stone-by-stone, she was tearing down the old and rebuilding a new foundation.

"Mom," Betts didn't often refer to her mother as "mom" but today the title seemed appropriate. "Look at your lovely table."

"Would you like coffee or lemonade this morning?" Lyla offered with a motherly smile. Her heart swelled hearing the title "mom" spill naturally from Betts's lips.

Betts took the offer of lemonade and the two decided to enjoy the sunshine in the chairs on the front porch. Lyla sat and patted the arm of Betts's chair, delighted to share her decision, "I've decided to go home to Beverly Hills, Betts. It's time."

Her mother's statement struck a sadness in Betts that she hadn't felt since the days she stood with her hand in Maybelle's as Lyla disappeared into a limousine leaving for a movie set somewhere far away. Betts felt too vulnerable to use the title of mom in the conversation now, "Oh but Mother, you promised to spend Easter with me."

"Betts, I wouldn't miss Easter with you for the world!" Lyla smiled at the reaction. She was overjoyed that her daughter wanted to spend time with her. "I'm not going to leave before then, but I am ready to go home. I'm feeling quite well and ready to begin working again on the projects I've left behind."

"Mom," Betts felt the conversation required the term of endearment again, "don't rush back into the same old schedule that put you here in the first place," she warned. "Remember, you have a heart condition and you must take care of yourself!"

"Bett's Knight, it's time for me to truly shine," Lyla declared. "I've been reading about the stars. Let me clarify, the stars in the sky, and did you know they burn brightest before they burn out and die."

"What are you saying to me, Mother? Do you know something I don't? Are you...are you?" Betts couldn't bring herself to utter the despairing next word.

"Oh, my goodness, no. I'm not dying, at least not yet!" Lyla was growing frustrated that her choice of words, while dramatic, were misunderstood, again. "On the contrary, I'm ready to shine brighter than ever!"

she explained. "I'm alive and breathing and I've been thinking God has given me another chance. I'm going to accept it as an opportunity to live life with passion! I don't want to just be passionate about acting, I want to be passionate about getting up in the morning and taking my next breath and next step and next bite of food. I want to be passionate about living."

"But what if you burn out as Lyla Fontaine? Maybe you could be passionate about living the restful, quiet life of Anne Knight, right here close to me and..."

Lyla stopped her daughter, "I would rather die in a blaze of glory than wither out somewhere obscure. The good Lord will take me when the time is right, whether tucked quietly away here in Arcadia or shining like a star in Hollywood."

Betts stood from her chair and leaned into her mother. With a hug she expressed her emotion, "Momma, I love you." It was a rare moment shared between the two, but a shining moment in Lyla's mind. "I wish you would stay in Florida so we could have lemonade together on sunny mornings more often, but you know I want the best for you." Betts felt like a parent sending a child off, "I'll get ahold of Judy and have her start making the arrangements to get you back to the mansion the week after Easter."

Lyla accompanied her daughter to her car and Betts dropped her oversized handbag onto the passenger's seat. Occasionally, she was forced to buckle the seat belt to keep the alarm in the car from beeping and flashing the warning that the passenger may be tossed through the windshield in a sudden and abrupt stop. With her notepads and books shoved into the bag for the meeting that day, this was one of those moments. She turned the key and the car alerted her to the heavy load in the seat next to her so she reached across and pulled the belt to the buckle. As she was preparing to leave, Smith whirred in behind her in the Club Car. He walked to Betts's window and stood next to Lyla.

Lyla greeted him, "Mr. Smith, this is my daughter, Reverend Betts Knight."

"Nice to meet you, Reverend Knight. I'll get out of your way, just wanted to say hello to my friend Anne's daughter that I've heard so much about." He smiled at Betts and she tried to place him in her mind. She had seen his face but couldn't recall where.

"Nice to meet you, Mr. Smith," Betts returned his smile.

"You are definitely your mother's daughter, two beauties." Smith stepped back to the golf cart. "We'll be at the pool soon, Anne, are you coming?"

Oh, what a schmoozer Betts thought, *maybe Hollywood is better for the great Lyla Fontaine.* She waved goodbye to her mother and nodded politely to Smith as she drove past him and turned in the direction of the Venus De

Milo. When she stopped at the traffic light and waited for a line of golf carts to parade across Highway 70, she noticed the cars in the parking lot in front of the diner, "That's it!" she said out loud, "Mr. Smith was the older gentleman in the diner." She gave herself kudos for remembering. The light turned green, the parade stopped, and Betts was back on the road to Fort Myers.

Chapter 21

The pool was quiet as Lyla laid her towel over the chaise lounge and settled into it quite comfortably, pressing the button on the armrest that raised her legs to a relaxed height. It had been a long while since she was poolside in public and was surprised by feeling self-conscious. Although accustomed to being in the limelight, poolside she was not wearing an Oscar De La Renta, nor had her makeup been artfully applied by her personal makeup artist. Lyla elected to keep her cover up on as she leaned back against the lumbar support hiding behind a floppy hat and bright blue sunglasses.

The ladies in the pool had finished their water aerobics class and hung on the pool edge while they chatted. Lyla listened for Village gossip, but nothing roused her curiosity. Sipping her lemonade, she watched the traffic on Highway 70 slow and stop at the light beyond the stucco wall then release and start up again. It was hard to imagine where the myriad of cars had come from or where their destinations would be, but Lyla decided it had to be somewhere beyond the city limits sign, the town of Arcadia was hardly a tourist draw surrounded by ranches and orange groves. She watched the cars slow, stop then start up again in the warmth of the sun and began to feel the heaviness of her eyelids behind her blue rimmed shades. The hum of cars and the whir of golf carts began to lull her into sleep until the rumble of a broken muffler startled her.

Lyla sat up straight in the chaise and pulled off her sunglasses. There at the stop light, fifty yards down the entrance lane to the Village and just beyond Venus De Milo was a rusty grey truck with a bare-armed man sitting in the driver's seat. She squinted to adjust her eyes in the bright sunlight. Distance kept her from getting a clear look to determine if he was the same flannel-clad hoodlum she and Betty had followed before, but she was sure it was the same truck. She stood to get a better look and noticed something different, the truck was dragging a trailer. No judge or jury would be needed, she was on to this fellow and as far as she was concerned, justice would prevail.

The light turned green and the engine of the truck drowned out the whir of the approaching golf cart. Betty and Smith arrived at the pool as the grey truck crossed the intersection and sped down the road with trailer attached, bouncing along behind. It drove past the four-foot wall and continued in the direction of the Low Land Palms Cattle Ranch.

Lyla pointed toward the truck and Betty leaned in close to Smith, "Take a good look boyfriend, that's probably going to be the get-away transportation for your Club Car in a few nights."

Smith winced, "Looks like she's probably not going to be riding in style."

It wasn't long before the pool area began to fill up with residents arriving for a cool after-lunch dip in the heat of the afternoon. The Willoughbys entered together and David called across the pool to Smith, "Thought that was your cart out there, mate. What are you doing here, aren't you going to open that golf course in a few days?"

"I'm just enjoying the afternoon with Betty while I wait for the installers to come and put up our sign. I'm ready to swing open the gates, man! We're set!" Smith called back. "Are you coming to the grand opening?"

"Wouldn't miss it!" David left Susan in the shade of an aqua-marine colored umbrella that covered a table and walked back out to the parking lot, "Wouldn't miss it for the world!" he shouted.

Dolores left the confines of the office and brought her sack lunch to the pool. She rolled up her capris and stood on the top step of the shallow end with her feet in the water to cool off. "Can I tell Leonard our little secret now, Betty or is it too soon?" She asked.

Betty wrinkled her forehead and cast a puzzled look in her direction.

"You remember how you came to the office to find out about your mysterious, handsome new neighbor. Or should I keep that quiet?" Dolores giggled.

Embarrassment flushed over Betty's cheeks. She sat frozen in the heat of the sun. Her mind raced for a reasonable explanation. The Lyla Fontaine secret was still under wraps and neither Lyla nor Smith knew of Betty's fact-finding mission with the "detective" Dolores Barnes in the Arcadia Retirement Village Office.

Smith however felt compelled to make the most of the situation, "Tell me more, Dolores. Please, tell me how my mysterious demeanor and boyish good looks drew the attention of the beautiful Betty Brown!"

Betty felt the flush travel from her cheeks to her toes. She shot Dolores a look over the top of her sunglasses that communicated nothing short of death if the conversation were to continue. "Dolores, please remember that you had an illegal hand in the filing cabinet that afternoon."

Dolores shrugged her shoulders, "Ahh yes, I was an accomplice. My lips are sealed."

Betty turned to Smith and glared, "Later," was all she said. He replied with a wink and a smirk.

Lyla kept one eye on the Village residents that came and went from the pool area and the other eye on Highway 70 hoping for the grey pick-up to return. She thought back to her Bond era and the adrenaline that coursed through her during the chase scenes. Although she knew she was never in any real danger, she would be overcome with excitement acting the part of the heroine. That same excitement rumbled around in her chest poolside in the Arcadia Retirement Village.

Feeling more confident, she decided to remove her cover-up, walk the length of the pool and dipped her toe in the cool water. William and Selma Bougher, still without their golf cart, walked to the pool and made their way to the hot tub. "Any news on the missing cart, yet?" Smith asked William.

"Nope, no sign of it. It hasn't turned up anywhere in the Village. We talked to Robby about it yesterday and he suggested we wait a few more days before we file a report."

Lyla turned to listen and shot a glance at Smith.

William noticed the exchange between the two and felt compelled to defend the officer, "I agreed with him. I hate to have the cost of my homeowner's insurance go up any higher. We had to fix a leak in the roof last fall and that did some damage to the budget already. Boy oh boy, they get you however they can."

Smith nodded in sympathy, "Well, as Robby always says, 'All's well that ends well.'"

Smith offered to spray SPF 50 on Betty's shoulders. She gladly accepted and handed him the sunscreen then turned her back for him to apply a steady stream. As Smith aimed and pushed the pump the rumble of the faulty muffler on the grey truck could be heard coming back down the road toward the intersection at the far end of the stucco wall. She snapped back to get a good look down Highway 70 just in time to get a mouthful of the sunscreen and began sputtering.

Lyla sprang from the pool edge as the truck came to a stop at the traffic light. She rushed to pat Betty's back as she gagged in the chaise lounge. Smith had dropped the spray can and it clanked and rolled into the pool. He grabbed Betty's bag in search of a water bottle, pulling out towels and her cell tossing them onto the chair beside him as she continued to choke and cough.

The pickup driver sat waiting for the red light to change to green at the intersection and noticed the movement taking place beyond the stucco wall. His eyes were drawn to the commotion and he turned his head in their direction. Smith standing with the still-sputtering Betty, dropped onto their chaise lounges out of his view, but Lyla donned her James Bond stance and stood squared in his direction. She pulled her sunglasses below the bridge of her nose and starred deliberately over the top of the blue frames.

"Ly...Anne, sit down, get down!" Betty whispered.

"It's him, it's the same dreadful man, Betty." Anne whispered back.

The light changed to green and the truck rumbled with the traffic through the intersection but this time without the trailer in tow. All eyes, poolside at the Arcadia Retirement Village were on Lyla, Betty, and Smith.

Herb Lewis, with his Village Manager name tag pinned neatly to his shirt pocket and Bootsie in his arms, had entered the pool area unnoticed during the commotion. He retrieved the spray can from the pool and handed it to Smith. "Is there a problem, Ms. Brown?"

Lyla, still in Bond mode, was first to respond, "That truck is a discredit to the Arcadia community. Such an awful rumble and noise. Aren't there laws and regulations that prohibit nuisances such as that, Mr. Lewis? Something should be done."

"Ms. Knight, my jurisdiction is the Retirement Village," Herb responded with an air of authority. "If I had the power to remove that driver from all roads, I certainly would but fortunately I was able to at least ban him from the Village."

"He would come here?" Betty asked innocently, "Whatever would a fellow like that, want in the Village?"

"Oh, he was doing some work for Mr. McCoy, but I put an end to them meeting here. I did not want that unsightly truck rumbling up and down our lanes," responded Herb raising his banner as Village Manager and protector of all things behind the stucco wall.

"Why thank you, Herb, I feel incredibly safe and secure with you in charge," Lyla purred.

Herb, with Bootsie tucked neatly in his arms walked a bit straighter as he turned to exit the pool and return to the office. "Enjoy the sun everyone!" he called over his shoulder drawing all attention to him and away from Lyla, Betty, and Smith. Conversation returned to the normal banter shifting between health topics and local gossip.

"Ellwood McCoy!" Smith said in a low voice, "I've been suspicious of ole Ellwood. I've seen him sit in the dark and watch the neighborhood at night. Something's fishy with that guy."

"On top of that, he has some tie to the flannel-wearing pick-up man," Lyla began. "Betty, you need to add that bit of information to your bullet points. And please note that the truck was pulling a trailer on the way out of town but returned without one."

Betty nodded, "Will do."

"Ladies, I think phase two of this wild operation has been quite successful," Smith surmised, "Quite successful indeed. I think I know how to dangle the Club Car like a carrot to lure our thief into our trap. But first I have a few things I need to put in place before the sting."

Chapter 22

The pole designed to hold the neon green sign had been secured days ago and stood ready to receive the LED billboard marking the entrance of the Putt-Putt. Smith stood with the foreman as it was lowered into place and wired for electricity. Before the final touches were managed by the Dorman Sign Company of South-Central Florida, Smith called Crystal. "We'll be flipping the switch in about a half hour, Crystal. I thought you might want to be here to witness the event."

"I'm on my way boss!" Crystal scrambled for her keys and jumped into her sky-blue Nissan she was able to purchase. Working for Leonard Smith was proving far more lucrative for the teen than earning tips at the Diner.

Smith made the same call to Betty and Lyla. They arrived moments later in the Porsche, which drew the attention of the Dorman Sign Company employees. A small group gathered outside the office in the parking lot with Smith ready to flip the switch when the signal came.

Two men in yellow golf shirts with Dorman Signs embroidered on the pocket asked to shake Lyla's hand and snap a selfie with her.

"Whatever for?" She asked innocently.

"Oh, come on, aren't you Lyla Fontaine?" the older of the two asked.

"You know, I get that all the time," she sighed and gave her spiel, "I just don't see the resemblance."

The elder didn't back down like most do and pushed for her confession, "I'd know if I was standing face-to-face with Lyla Fontaine, you can't fool me. What in the world are you doing driving a Porsche through Arcadia, Florida Ms. Fontaine? Are you filming here, at one of the ranches?"

Lyla answered apologetically, "Sir, I'm sorry to disappoint you but my name is Anne. I live here in the Arcadia Retirement Village. Leonard is a friend of mine..."

But the fan still pressed, "What's going on here, is this some kind of TV prank?"

Betty stepped between the two men and Lyla, "Could you please get back to work and leave my friend alone. We're just here to see Claire's Putt-Putt Golf in lights, thank you very much."

They complied momentarily and completed the task of carrying tools back to the work van but returned to Lyla's side with a third co-worker. "I told you, it's Lyla Fontaine!" insisted the elder.

The third man in the yellow golf shirt stuck out his hand and offered it to Lyla, "How do you do, Ma'am. I'm a huge fan, I couldn't get enough of James Bond. It was a crying shame when they dumped you and hired that younger actress to take your place."

That was all Lyla could take, "Where is your foreman and why aren't you working? I'm feeling a bit uncomfortable with this conversation. Excuse me." She made her way into the office and disappeared out of sight.

The men on the job continued to speculate why Lyla Fontaine would be at a Putt-Putt in Arcadia, Florida, when one of them remarked that the owner looked an awful lot like the PGA golfer Smith Kennedy. The foreman interrupted the conversation and hollered, "Ready? Okay flip the switch!" and the lime green light blazed *Claire's Putt-Putt Golf Course.*

Crystal let out a whoop and applauded, "Idn't that the prettiest sign you ever did see? I love it, boss, I just love it!"

"Congratulations, Smith," Betty smiled with great admiration and patted his forearm, "I know your wife would have been honored to have her name up on that sign. It's a lovely tribute to her."

Smith turned away. He was astonished at the well of emotion bubbling within him and blinked to keep the moisture forming in his eyes from rolling down his cheek. "This is for you, love. I sure miss you," he whispered with eyes turned upward.

The men gathered their tools and packed them into the company van and Lyla remained out of sight in the Putt-Putt office watching from Smith's chair she had rolled near the window. She reminisced about the tribute paid to her at Grauman's Chinese theater thirty-some years earlier. It seemed a grand affair at the time but today it paled in comparison to the tribute Smith made to his wife.

Lyla had pressed her hands into soft cement, looked into the camera and smiled revealing the small space between her teeth. Light bulbs flashed and the press wrote stories to appear in newspapers around the globe. Her name in bronze was embedded into the star and a veil was pulled back that day revealing it cemented to the sidewalk as her fans cheered. But it wouldn't be long before someone younger, prettier and more talented would woo her Hollywood fans and she would be forgotten. Another blond Bond girl would take the lead and Lyla's movies would be archived on some obscure cable network for the lonely and forlorn to discover while silently surfing channels on sleepless nights. Then, lighting on Lyla's movies, they would be reminded of how small their lives had been, falling far short of heroic adventure and epic love. "My goodness, how sad is my legacy," Lyla sighed.

And then she thought of Claire. Claire was enshrined in a lime green beacon of hope. Her name blazed in neon at the spot where families would play together, where young hearts would fall in love, where friends would gather to laugh and blow off steam at the end of a hard day. Claire's name would be synonymous with joy; pure Putt-Putt joy! Lyla imagined mothers saying to fathers, *Let's take the kids to Claire's* or co-workers planning a trip to Claire's on Friday night. Her name would live on through the memories of every Putt-Putt golfer smacking a golf ball through the giant windmill or into the mouth of the hippopotamus and all because her sign was hung as a symbol of eternal adoration; a reflection of lives lived in love.

Lyla never found that kind of love on a movie set. She thought she had fallen for Betts's father and from time to time regretted not marrying him when he proposed, but she knew he was acting out of obligation, not love. Their story most likely would not have persevered the years nor ended as sweetly as Smith and Claire's.

Crystal barged through the office door and gathered her car keys, interrupting Lyla's thoughts, "You okay

Ms. Anne? I saw you come in here when those guys were givin' you a hard time."

"Thank you, Crystal, yes, I'm fine. I just needed a drink of cold water out of the sun, that's all." Lyla reached for her water bottle as she spoke justifying her little white lie.

Crystal continued to question, "What were they buggin' you about, Ma'am? I didn't like you getting all flustered like that."

Lyla felt her frustration level rising again so she rolled her eyes and huffed a cliché, "Oh, boys will be boys, no matter how old they get."

"Who were they thinkin' you were?" Crystal quizzed.

Lyla didn't care to continue this vein of conversation and wanted to move it in another direction, "Are you ready for the grand opening tomorrow?" she asked. Then, hoping Crystal would be thrown off subject easier than the Dorman Sign employees she turned to praise, "Leonard says you've been absolutely indispensable. He has just raved about your natural abilities in dealing with people."

Crystal followed Lyla's subject change, "I just love workin' here, he's the best boss I've ever had. Course I only had one other, Roy at the diner," she giggled, "but Mr. Smith is the best. See you tomorrow at the Grand Opening, Ma'am." Crystal bounced down the steps and over to her Nissan.

Smith found Lyla in the office viewing the scene from the window. She stood and slipped her arm in his as a gesture of friendship and support, "Your wife was a lucky woman to be loved so deeply, Smith."

"No, I was the lucky one," he countered.

Outside in the parking lot one of the yellow-shirted men could be heard saying, "I heard she had a heart attack or something. No one knows where she is. Maybe she died."

Truck doors were slammed shut and the crew pulled out of the parking lot and were gone.

Betty stormed through the office door, "That older fellow wouldn't give up!"

"I'm sorry to have left you two but I had to come inside to avoid the Dorman Sign paparazzi," Lyla sighed, relieved the ordeal was over.

"Out of sight, out of mind, hopefully they'll forget about the Lyla sighting," Betty offered optimistically.

Smith straightened some things on his desk, checked the window locks and prepared to leave the Putt-Putt. Tomorrow would prove to be a long day. "Come on Betty, it's time for the show to continue. Would you like a ride home, girlfriend?" He locked the office as the three stepped into the parking lot. Above them the lime green sign hummed quietly and glowed as the sun was beginning to set. "It's a beautiful sight, isn't it? I think sweet Claire is getting her chance to shine again," Smith beamed.

Smith and Betty followed the golf cart path along Highway 70 past the Piggly Wiggly. Lyla had climbed into the Porsche and buckled the seat belt before she noticed a piece of paper stuck under her windshield wiper. With the window rolled down she tried to reach across the windshield but couldn't stretch far enough even after she unbuckled her seat belt. The thought crossed her mind to just ignore the scrap and she was tempted to leave it between wiper and glass but decided she couldn't bear the guilt if it went wafting down the road through traffic. She huffed and climbed back out of the Porsche to reach the paper. On it was written:

WE KNOW WHO YOU ARE LYLA FOUNTAINE
HOW MUCH WILL YOU PAY TO KEEP IT SECRET
WE'LL FIND YOU

Although the note was threatening, the words didn't frighten Lyla, she had dealt with scoundrels her entire career. However, she was highly annoyed no punctuation had been used in the scrawled threat and her last name was misspelled. *If some thug is going to threaten me, he should at least be professional about it,* she mused.

The Dorman Sign employees knew where she lived by her adamant confession that she was Anne and a resident of the Arcadia Retirement Village so, of course, if they meant business, they could find her. But in her estimation, this seemed to be a fan just trying to smoke out Lyla Fontaine. Most threats, in her recollection, never amounted to much and she would be back in Hollywood soon, anyway. She tucked the note into the glove box on the dash.

Smith punched in his code at the gate and the two made a full circle of the Village before he took Betty home. Smith in his golf cap and Betty with her dyed auburn hair blowing romantically in the wind, made a lovely couple. The girls in Blanche's posse made a full report and spread the word that Betty spent the afternoon at the Putt-Putt supporting the widower at the unveiling of "The Sign."

Chapter 23

When Claire's Putt-Putt Golf Course opened its doors to Putt-Putt enthusiasts, Crystal Bell was proven correct. Hole 15, the giant, golf ball eating, hippo, was a crowd favorite. Children begged their parents to play again and again just to see the huge mouth lift, devour the ball, then deposit it with gusto out of the far end of the mechanical animal.

Macho Nacho Mexican Cuisine arrived in plenty of time to inflate the giant sombrero atop the orange food truck. A line formed and wound around the parking lot but Johnny, the owner and head cook, was prepared to deliver plenty of delicious nachos, tacos, and burritos just as he promised, hot and fast. With every order completed the young lady at the counter would shout, "Ole!"

Mounds of fifteen different flavors of ice cream were scooped into cones and bowls at the *Smooth Southern Ice-Cold Treats* counter. A small "fixings bar" was accessible on a table that folded out from the side of the truck and customers added sprinkles, chopped nuts, and maraschino cherries atop their favorite flavors creating a mountain of scrumptious delight.

Families trekked from the far corners of DeSoto County in cars, vans, and buses, all toting hopeful Putt-Putters willing to wait in line for their turn to play the course. They arrived in town driving under banners draped streetlight-to-streetlight across the main roads announcing the up-coming dates of the *All Florida Championship Rodeo*. Children squealed with delight and parents clutched their bank cards. Arcadia buzzed with excitement.

Late afternoon as the crowd at Claire's Putt-Putt began to overflow from the course to the parking lot, Smith noticed a group pointing at him and whispering. A couple of golfers asked for a selfie and his autograph. He rambled the same spiel to everyone asking if he were Smith Kennedy, "Sorry, I guess some folks think we look alike, I don't really see the resemblance. I'm Leonard, the owner, thanks for coming to try your skills on the course." He decided, if he wanted to conceal his identity, he would have to follow Lyla's example from the previous day and hide in the Putt-Putt office.

Betty and Lyla had made a couple of passes through the parking lot in the Porsche but couldn't find an available spot, so they parked at the Piggly Wiggly and followed the glow of the lime green sign across Mary

Jean Drive to Claire's Putt-Putt Golf Course. Crystal Bell was busy helping waiting golfers choose the color of ball each wanted to whack and the right size club to whack it with. Her friend, and hired co-worker was accepting cash and credit cards at the counter, while other teens and young adults manned the four corners of the course. Lyla waved to her from behind a family of crying preschoolers as the father tried to explain that only one pink ball could be used each game and the other players must choose a ball of a different color.

"Where's the boss?" Betty yelled above the sobs.

"Office," was all Crystal could manage to shout back. The talkative teen had met her match in the little group of dismayed golfers.

The two women worked their way through the crowd and up the stairs to the office door. Lyla knocked, "Hellooo? Are you in there, Smith?"

He opened the door and hurried them in, "I've been recognized, get in here!" He shut the door behind them. "I wouldn't mind the marketing advantage of having my name associated with the Putt-Putt course, but I don't want to attract attention until we get this golf cart dilemma solved. We've come this far; I want to see it to the end."

Betty chimed in, "We had better make it happen soon; Lyla was recognized yesterday and you today, it won't be long until the press shows up."

"I've been thinking about the timing," Lyla began, "and I think the first night of the rodeo will be the perfect time to catch the cart-nabbers. Any greedy thief will find it irresistible to work under the veil of all the excitement and commotion in the Village. With so much activity, he'll jump at the chance to swipe a cart that's been left in the open."

"Betty, I've been thinking about this. What if you and I go to the Club House that evening for a picnic. Can you fix a picnic dinner?" Smith asked.

"I can manage that," Betty replied.

He continued in a very business-like tone, pacing in the office, "We'll sit at one of the umbrella tables and enjoy the sunset while the Villagers buzz past on their way to the rodeo. If the crook is as studious of his surroundings as I think he is, he'll notice we're there alone and as the Village empties, he'll come back to check on the Club Car."

Lyla turned up the volume of her James Bond persona, "Smith, the other day you said you had thought of a way to dangle the Club Car like a carrot, so tell us your plan."

He took a final step in his pacing and swung his body around to face the two ladies, "I just did, Lyla."

"That's it? Lyla blurted out, "That's not a carrot, Smith, that's a radish. Who wants a radish? Radishes aren't tempting. This thief must be lured and teased beyond what he can bear. He's got to know that the Club Car is his for the taking that night. We are going to have to be far more deliberate in our offering him the chance to steal it, than that flimsy plan of yours, for goodness sake."

"I've got it," Betty jumped up, "I've got it! We just need to get the news to Ellwood McCoy's ears. He needs to know that you and I are having a picnic and watching the sunset instead of going to the rodeo. Then, when we walk home past his house and look all lovey dovey, he'll know we left the Club Car behind. And guess what? He'll give the word to his cronies to come pick it up ASAP. You can bet your cowboy boots he'll have someone there to nab it before the last bull is ridden at the rodeo and the residents are all headed home for bed."

Smith nodded approvingly of the plan but thought of an essential detail that needed to be ironed out, "If we leave the Club House and walk home past ole Ellwood's cottage, how do we get a picture of the thief taking the Club Car?"

"We'll just hide behind the stucco wall," Lyla offered.

"Oh, Lyla, that's a bit obvious. Someone will see us and ask what we're doing," Betty protested.

Lyla continued, "There's an empty bungalow with a backyard that borders the wall. I just saw Herb put a For Sale sign in the yard yesterday. After you two stroll hand-in-hand to Betty's, we'll take our lawn chairs and camera over there, duck down behind the wall and wait."

Betty continued her protest, "Someone is sure to see us."

"No," Smith corrected, "We'll time it right and it will be dark. Then, we'll change into dark clothes and blend into the night," he added in a rather mysterious tone.

"Camouflaged!" Lyla exclaimed with delight. "Oh yes!"

"Ellwood won't see us, he'll be too busy calling his flannel-shirted buddy to notice us, and if we keep our timing right the other neighbors will either be at the rodeo or watching Jeopardy," Smith added. He was enjoying this secret agent identity that was rising within him.

"We certainly won't miss the pick-up; we'll know when that noisy, old grey truck stops at the gate." Lyla paused and opened her eyes wide as she continued her thought, "I'll bet he'll use Ellwood's code to raise the gate and get in!"

"Yes! That's it!" Smith agreed. "That's how he's been getting in and out of the Village."

Lyla completed the plan with a final step, "Then, when the Club Car is on the trailer and headed out of the Village, we'll snap a picture and call Officer Robertson."

"Yes!" agreed Smith again, then immediately countered, "No! Wait just a minute. We've got to be sure we know where they're taking my Club Car?"

"Robby will be on it," Lyla answered with enthusiasm. "We'll provide the Arcadia Police Department with the proof it's been taken, and they'll chase down the criminals. We'll do our part and they'll do the rest, Smith."

Crystal Bell bounced through the door interrupting the conversation, "Best day ever, boss! We're makin' a killing out there. Didn't I tell you the hippo would bring 'em in?"

"You sure did, Kiddo," Smith patted the teen on the back, "I'd better stick with you, Partner."

Chapter 24

Opening day of the *All Florida Championship Rodeo* brought crowds from cities all over the state. The town of Arcadia was overflowing with bronco busters, barrel racers, and steer wrestlers. Jake "The Jerk" Sampson, overall winner from the previous year, was surrounded by fans in the Piggly Wiggly parking lot signing autographs. He tucked his shirt in behind his championship belt buckle and strutted proudly snapping selfies with anyone who asked. Even Dolores returned to the Arcadia Retirement Village with a picture of "The Jerk" displayed as new wallpaper on her cell phone.

The rodeo officially opened at 4:00 p.m. with the playing and singing of the National Anthem. The sound system, when cranked to top volume, echoed beyond the walls of the arena and could be heard all through the city of Arcadia including the Retirement Village. Local vocalist, Jolene Swanson, won the opportunity to perform the anthem with the South Florida Marching

Band at a talent search held in Fort Myers Beach, beating out 243 other applicants. At first note, the residents of the Retirement Village gathered outside their homes to listen with their hands placed over their hearts and eyes cast skyward. Reverend Frank Tilby of the New Life Southern Baptist Church followed Jolene to the microphone and offered a moving invocation beseeching the Lord to protect the cowboys and cowgirls as they bravely faced the challenges before them.

Judges were introduced, and housekeeping announcements were up next on the schedule. It was during these announcements that the Villagers gathered their tickets, bottled water, cowboy hats and sunglasses to board the Arcadia Retirement Village People Mover for a ride to the arena. The fifteen-passenger van would make several trips from the Village to the DeSoto County Rodeo Arena, leaving from the Club House about every fifteen minutes. It would be an hour before the first event would officially begin giving everyone plenty of time to get through the ticket gate and make their way to the grandstands. Most of the Villagers elected to ride the people mover rather than pay for parking at the rodeo arena.

Smith and Betty drove the Club Car past Ellwood McCoy's cottage and waved hello rather obnoxiously to be sure to draw his attention as they jockeyed into position. Arriving at the Club House, Betty chose a table with an aqua-marine umbrella next to a stately king palm tree in clear view of the boarding area. She opened their picnic dinner as the first wave of residents stood waiting for their ride. Many called hello to them or asked if they would be coming along later.

Smith answered confidently every time the People Mover reloaded, "Not tonight, we just wanted a quiet evening under the stars."

As the two leisurely dined on fried chicken and pasta salad, Betty realized how pleasant Smith could be and she began to appreciate their conversation. Picnicking together was turning out to be a rather enjoyable first step in the plan they had all agreed on for the stake out. Since she wasn't really his girlfriend, and this wasn't really a date, both felt at ease and their conversation turned easily from the weather to a more intimate exchange. They were like two old classmates reuniting and recounting life's milestones.

Smith spoke freely to Betty about Claire. It had been a long time since he had allowed himself to express his sorrow of living alone and the loneliness that engulfed him in the evening hours. Claire's name glowing in lime green, shown down on him like a beacon and rekindled the memory of her. He leaned forward in his chair and confessed how he longed for her voice and her touch again.

Betty felt compelled to take his hand and urge him to tell her more. She listened intently to his memories as he described in detail how he and Claire had met and fallen in love. "She was a beautiful woman with a heart as big as the sky," Smith told Betty, "and her eyes just as blue."

He talked for over an hour about their life together before he glanced at his wristwatch. "I'm so sorry, Betty, I have gone on and on, I can't believe you've let me ramble for an hour. Can you forgive me for monopolizing the conversation?" Smith realized how much he appreciated this newfound friendship, "You are just so easy to talk to, a great listener, and you've let me drone on. But, what about you? Have you ever married?"

Betty's eyes dropped and a sadness visibly swept over her.

"I'm sorry, am I being too personal?" Smith questioned.

"I was married once, for almost eighteen months. My husband, Carl, loved riding Highway 1 along the coast on his motorcycle. One afternoon he was caught in a downpour and lost control on a curve. I loved him more than anything else in this world and I felt as though my life ended with his. Depression gripped my heart so deeply I thought I couldn't live. For many weeks, no months, I battled that pain and the desire to jump off one of those cliffs and join Carl. I've always carried the guilt that I had turned down his offer to ride with him that day. I was just too busy doing housework! Can you believe I wasn't there for him because I needed to vacuum?"

Betty fell silent and Smith squeezed her hand still in his, "I decided I would never hurt like that again so I threw myself into managing the careers of Lyla Fontaine and many other Hollywood stars and I never looked back. He's been gone an awfully long time but even after all these years, when I allow myself the pleasure to think about him, my heart still aches for that man."

"I'm sorry, Betty, I didn't know. I can't begin to imagine how devastated you must have been, so young and alone..." Smith's voice trailed off. He felt his heart break under the weight of Betty's pain, "Lyla never told me your story."

"She doesn't know," Betty confessed, "I never told anyone. When I began my career, I believed my history would not be appropriate information for the workplace. The longer I kept silent the easier it was to just push the pain deeper. And Smith, I just knew I couldn't endure their pathetic sympathy and gestures of understanding. No one can understand, I don't understand it myself and I was the one who lived through it."

"Why did you tell me?" Smith asked quietly.

"Because you put up that great, big, lime green sign, that's why." Betty smiled, "The moment it lit up I knew you had known love with Claire like I had known with Carl."

The two sat in silence for a long while and watched the Florida sun begin to sink slowly into the western sky while hoots and hollers came through the sound system at the All Florida Championship Rodeo.

The pink and orange Florida sunset began to deepen to purple. Smith and Betty knew the task that lay before them, so they gathered what was left of the picnic into the basket, shut the lid and hand-in-hand began to walk to Betty's bright yellow cottage. The melancholy mood set at the picnic under the aqua-marine umbrella was broken knowing they had to strategically work the plan.

Smith shattered their silence in a loud jovial voice forced for the occasion, "That was a wonderful dinner, my dear. Let's walk home and enjoy the night sky. I'll get the Club Car tomorrow morning."

"How wonderfully romantic," Betty chimed back. "I need a good walk."

They laughed out loud as they passed Ellwood McCoy's cottage. Smith whistled a happy tune for a few steps before shouting in amazement, "Will you look at that Florida sky! It's a beauty tonight."

"It's getting dark," Betty sang out, "Let's go sit out at my place and watch the stars come out."

To Betty's dismay, Ellwood hadn't been sitting on his front porch when the two passed by, but Smith reassured her, "Oh, he was there. There was quiet movement in the carport."

"Well, I hope it was him and not the neighbor's cat," Betty sighed.

Lyla's phone buzzed with a text message: *Meet us at the wall* followed by a thumbs up emoji indicating all had gone as expected.

Lyla bound her silver curls in a black silk scarf and stepped into a black jumpsuit and matching booties purchased off the rack at Neiman Marcus. Although, buying off the rack wasn't her norm, she believed it wouldn't be an issue for a stake out. Avoiding the street lights that were beginning to buzz in the twilight, she took the short trek across the street with a dark rucksack on her back containing a couple of bottles of water, her cell phone and a second dark scarf to wrap around her shoulders should she get chilled in the night air.

With most residents at the rodeo cheering for Jake The Jerk, Lyla moved easily between shadowy cottages avoiding those with windows aglow from the light of a big screen TV blaring the voice of Alex Trebec. She carried three navy blue, low sitting, beach chairs sporting white anchors on the back cushion that were purchased earlier in the week. They would serve the purpose of keeping the waiting detectives off the damp ground but still concealed behind the stucco and when the sting was over, she would use them at a villa somewhere along the Pacific coast.

The house with the For Sale sign was near the end of the four-foot tall stucco wall closest to Highway 70. *The perfect spot,* Lyla thought as she placed the three new chairs neatly lined against the stucco. Looking over the wall to her left Lyla had a clear view down the exit lane to the Village gate, out on the boulevard in front of her rose the Venus De Milo, like a Roman Sentry in position to guard the three on their gallant mission. Finally, to her right, she was slightly hidden behind the giant seashell but could clearly see the traffic light on the corner of Highway 70. Satisfied with her position, she lowered herself into the recently purchased beach chairs, removed her phone from the pack and prepared to wait.

Betty and Smith arrived only moments later. Betty had changed from her peach picnic wear to black spandex yoga pants and a long sleeve purple and black t-shirt paired with her tennis shoes; in case they would have to move quickly.

"Yoga pants? I have never seen you in yoga pants, Betty. What possessed you to make such a purchase, dear?" Lyla was glad it was twilight, hoping Betty wouldn't catch sight of her facial expression and rolled her eyes.

"Lyla, they're designed to hold one's softer parts tightly in place. I certainly do not want parts of me bouncing out of place tonight. That would not be a very pretty sight," Betty explained.

Smith was in black jeans and black polo with lime green glow-in-the-dark lettering spelling out *Claire's Putt-Putt Golf* across the back.

"Smith, someone will see the billboard on your backside! Sit down!" Lyla commanded in a whisper.

Betty opened a bag of potato chips and offered them around.

"I thought you two just had dinner?" Lyla whispered again.

"Yes, and it was a lovely dinner, but I always eat when I'm nervous," Betty confessed.

Lyla was growing impatient, "I hope you both understand this is a stake out, not happy hour at the club, now sit down and keep your eyes and ears open."

The three sat silently behind the stucco for a long while waiting to hear the rumble of the rusty grey truck. Instead, they heard the distant voice of the commentator at the rodeo over the loudspeaker cut through the night. Soft purring car engines rolled up and down highway 70 and they counted a dozen sets of headlights moving above the wall as they continued to wait.

Chapter 25

Smith was the first to hear it, but it wasn't the rumble of the cranky old muffler, it was the quiet whir of a golf cart. "Listen," he whispered, "That's my golf cart, that's the Club Car. Someone is driving my Club Car."

"Are you sure?" Betty asked quietly. "How can you be sure that's your golf cart?"

"Just trust me, I know that's her!" Smith raised slightly and looked down the exit lane. The headlights were stopped, waiting as the gate lifted. "And she's about to leave the Village without me!"

All three rose from the chairs but remained crouched out of sight behind the stucco. One after another they raised their heads to peek over the top. The Club Car was whirring toward the seashell sign bidding it *Goodbye Please Drive Safely* as it approached Highway 70.

Smith raised the volume of his whisper, "Get a picture, get a picture!"

The cart slowed at the speed bump giving Betty the perfect shot. She snapped a picture with her cell and the flash blinked in the night. All three dropped to their knees and held their breaths as their hearts bumped in their chests. The Club Car stopped.

"Who's there?" hissed a voice from beyond the stucco wall.

The loudspeaker announced the next bronco buster and the crowd cheered but not a sound could be heard from either side of the stucco wall. Frozen and silent, the trio crouched out of sight, their heads tucked well below the top of the wall.

A faint rumble of a rusted muffler and clatter of an empty trailer could be heard on Highway 70 coming from beyond the Putt-Putt and approaching the Village entrance. The Club Car remained silent as the pickup rumbled to a stop at the traffic light. "Get ready for another picture," Lyla whispered, "The truck will turn this way when the light turns green."

But instead, the truck turned the opposite direction into the Walmart parking lot and stopped outside the diner. The Club Car whirred past the Venus De Milo to the traffic light. Smith jumped up and held his finger on the shutter control button of his cell taking a burst of photos before the cart reached the far side of the intersection.

Betty took full advantage of her spandex and tennis shoes and sprang into action. She grabbed Lyla's black scarf and made her way to the portion of the stucco wall that ran parallel to the highway. She concealed her head and bravely rose above the height of the wall, adorned in her black-camouflaged glory, and videotaped the Club Car being driven onto the trailer attached to the grey pickup. She was able to get a good look at the license plate as she filmed: GRG 7559

Crawling back to Lyla and Smith, Betty whispered above the noise of the muffler as it waited to turn back onto Highway 70, "Call Robby, call Robby! I've got it, I have all the evidence right here! Same truck, same license plate! Just call and tell him, 'Lock 'em up!'"

Smith was fiddling with something on his phone and said, "Quick, Lyla, you call while I get this started."

Lyla dialed 911, "What are you starting at a time like this, Smith?"

"I hid a tracking device under the dash of the Club Car. It's connected to an app on my phone. I am not going to wait for Robby to bury this report. I'll track it down myself if I have to."

"Arcadia Police, is this an emergency?"

"Yes, it is, my friend's golf cart was stolen," Lyla informed the dispatcher.

"Your location please?" asked the voice over the phone.

"Well, we're currently hiding behind the stucco wall at the Arcadia Retirement Village. We just witnessed it leaving the Village."

"Are you sure the owner wasn't driving, Ma'am?"

"YES! I'm absolutely sure! He's here with me behind the wall, but his golf cart is being toted down the road on a trailer that is connected to an unsightly and very loud grey pickup truck. You can't miss it; the hideous hunk of rust should be banned from the streets!" Lyla exclaimed emphatically.

There was silence on the other end.

"Helloooo, are you there?" Lyla yelled into the phone. "We have pictures and a video of the whole operation. Do you hear me?"

The voice mumbled something to someone other than Lyla.

"HEY! We need you to get in your cruiser and go get that golf cart with lights flashing and siren wailing, if you please!" Lyla, who normally shuttered at the use of declaratives such as 'Hey', had lost her patience with the dispatcher.

"Officer Robertson is currently on duty at the rodeo, Ma'am, but I'll have him stop by your home first thing in the morning to take a report. Can I have your name and address?"

"Lyla Fon..."

"NO!" Betty yelled.

Lyla stopped, took a quick breath and began again, "This is Anne Knight on Sunset Lane but tomorrow will be too late. The cart is currently traveling out of town on Highway 70, thank you very much." She hung up exasperated with the dispatcher.

"Thank you for stopping me Betty," Lyla said discouraged, "but they aren't coming."

"Oh no!" Betty gasped.

"I know," Smith shook his head, "this is not turning out like we expected! That thief is getting away with my Club Car!"

"NO! NO! NO!" Betty exclaimed, "Look at this picture!" she held out her phone and Lyla and Smith huddled around her. The three stood in silent astonishment. Betty had snapped a picture of the golf cart approaching them and discovered a clear view of the driver.

"That's David Willoughby," Lyla gasped.

"I'm not letting that lunatic drive off with my Club Car." Smith shouted, "Lyla, get your keys."

"WHAT? What are you thinking, Smith Kennedy?" Betty questioned as she grabbed for the beach chairs.

"I'm chasing him down!" Smith doggedly replied, "I'm not going to just stand here trapped behind four feet of stucco while David Willoughby escapes with my Club Car. I'm going after him!"

"Well, you're not going alone, Smith, he could be armed and dangerous! You could be injured, or worse! And then you'll end up on national news!" Lyla cried out dramatically as the three scurried down Sunset Lane.

"I'm not going to confront the guy, I'm not nuts," Smith said huffing, "but I am going to get his location. My tracker has him heading down Highway 70 toward the city limits." He deposited the chairs into Lyla's carport.

Lyla and Betty scurried up the steps and into the cottage to grab the keys to the Porsche. "Betty, I can't go another step, my nerves have me ready to burst! If we're going to be chasing crooks into all hours of the night, I will be far more effective if I jump in here first," Lyla confessed to Betty closing the bathroom door behind her.

"Well then, I'm next!" Betty said as she waited.

Smith tapped his foot on the driveway while he checked the tracking device on his phone. Losing his patience, he finally barged into the cottage, "What in the world is taking so long? My golf cart may be halfway across the state by now."

Lyla stood in the dinette with car keys in hand. Betty called from behind a door, "I'll be out in a minute, I'll be especially quick in my spandex!"

"OH geez!" Smith dropped his shoulders and rolled his eyes.

"We won't have to stop along the way," Lyla promised, "We're down to business now."

The team of crime-busters squeezed into the Porsche. "We really can't take this car, you know," Betty said, as Lyla was backing out of the drive. "It's far too conspicuous and David Willoughby will know it's us."

"She's right," Smith agreed. Lyla shifted the gears from reverse to forward and pulled back under the carport. "But, on the other hand, this is all we have, and I want my Club Car back," Smith reasoned. Lyla shifted the Porsche back into reverse and inched out onto Sunset Lane a second time. Waiting for Smith to change his mind again, she put the car in neutral and idled in the middle of the street to discuss the next step.

"We can track the golf cart," Smith said, "and just find out where it's being taken, then call the Police Department again."

"But they will recognize the Porsche," Betty countered again, "and that could be dangerous. We can take my car," Lyla pushed the gear shift into forward preparing to pull it back into the carport, "but I'm almost on empty so we'll need to fill up."

"We don't have the time for pumping gas," Smith shook his head as he spoke.

Lyla put the Porsche in park and sat in the middle of the road watching for traffic as Smith and Betty debated the best course of action. As she listened to their banter, she was quite pleased that she had slipped into the lady's room knowing it was going to be a long night. She watched the road for oncoming headlights, however, instead of an approaching vehicle she could see a husky figure walking toward them in the dark avoiding the streetlights. She interrupted shouting frantically, "Here comes someone! What are we going to do?"

"We need another car, get to the Putt-Putt! Now!" Smith demanded.

The Porsche shifted into drive almost hitting the dark figure ahead of them. As they swerved past, all three immediately recognized Ellwood McCoy. Lyla gasped and Betty screamed as they rounded the corner and headed out of the Village, past the Venus De Milo.

"Venus! I hope we live to see you again," yelled Betty to the statue in her cowboy hat as they dodged the speed bump and ran the red light.

Ellwood was on his phone, "Tell Robby we got trouble. The movie star, the golfer, and the normal one are all jammed into the Porsche and up to something. I'm thinking it may not turn out so good if you don't get them stopped. I think they may be following Benny."

Chief Norton gave Ellwood a command from the other end of the phone, "Follow that Porsche and don't let them out of your sight."

Lyla slammed on her brakes in the Putt-Putt parking lot. Smith jumped from the passenger's side and found Crystal. "We need your help, Crystal, we need your car, it's an emergency! Are your keys in the office?"

"Well, I'm not allowed to let anyone else drive it according to my dad and my insurance guy," Crystal explained apologetically.

Smith tried his best to calmly give Crystal the *Cliff Notes* version of the situation, "Listen Crystal, this is an emergency and we've got no time to lose. Someone has heisted my Club Car. I put a tracking device under the dash and I'm still getting a reading but if we don't get going, we're going to lose the signal. We really need your car because the guy that swiped my Club Car will recognize the Porsche."

"Holy cats, boss! I'm in, let's go get him! You all jump in my Nissan and I'll drive ya." Crystal called to the worker behind the counter, "Got an emergency, we'll be back."

She pushed the unlock button on her key fob and said, "Come on, y'all are wasting a lot of time just standin' around here."

With no other option, the three climbed into the sky-blue Nissan, Smith up front with Crystal, Lyla and Betty in the back seat. "We can chase all the crooks you want," Crystal explained as she pulled to the road, "but I have a strict rule, no eating in my car. I just can't stand little crumbs all over."

Betty returned her half-eaten bag of chips to her purse.

Ellwood McCoy could see the silver Porsche in the Putt-Putt parking lot from Highway 70 and kicked up stones as he pulled in. Keeping his eyes on the car in front of him he never saw Crystal pulling out of the parking lot and turning onto Highway 70 in the direction Smith was pointing.

"Lyla, did you see that?" Betty whispered.

"See what?" Crystal asked.

"Nothing important, dear," Lyla fibbed to Crystal but mouthed the words *Ellwood McCoy* to Betty.

The tracking signal on Smith's phone was growing weak, "Sorry Crystal, you need to speed up, I'm losing the signal."

"Okay folks, what's going on here?" the young driver asked.

There was silence from the back seat so Crystal demanded an answer, "Boss, come on, you can trust me, and you know it. What's up?"

Smith sucked in a deep breath, "Crystal, here's my promise; I'll gladly tell you the whole story after we find out where the crooks have taken my Club Car but right now I just need you to concentrate on driving."

"It's a deal, boss, but I just gotta know, does this have anything to do with you being the pro golfer Smith Kennedy, you gotta trust me and tell me the truth." Crystal didn't take her eyes off the road, but Smith could see her expression. She deserved the truth.

"Yes, Crystal Bell, it does," Smith confessed.

"My dad is gonna freak out!" she squealed.

"How did you find out?" Smith questioned but continued on before she could answer, "Hey, the signal is getting stronger. Looks like they are headed into Zolfo Springs."

Crystal drove the trio of detectives past the Arcadia city limits sign, "You know, I expected somethin' was up as we got closer to opening the Putt-Putt. A whole lot of folks were askin' me about you and what it was like workin' for a genuine golf pro. But boss, I didn't tell any of 'em askin' anything and I didn't say nothin' to you about it cuz I figured if you wanted me to know, you'd a told me." Crystal glanced at her boss then returned her eyes to the road ahead of her.

"So, you just didn't ask me? Even though you suspected I wasn't who I said I was?" Smith questioned Crystal.

"Yup, you're a great boss and I didn't worry cuz I figured you had your reasons. Then when you put up that lime green sign, I knew I'd never have to worry at all workin' for a boss who was filled up so full of love like you."

The ladies in the back seat broke into the conversation in wholehearted agreement, "She's right, Smith." Betty embellished, "Any man who would pay tribute to his deceased wife like you is far from a threat!"

"But then tonight a reporter guy from a paper I've never heard of stopped at the Putt-Putt," Crystal continued.

"What?" Lyla asked with trepidation in her voice. "A reporter?"

"Do you remember the name of the paper?" Betty asked.

"I think it was somethin' with initials, E, G something," she answered.

Lyla broke in, "That's E.E.G., Exclusive Entertainment Gossip. They won't stop until they find me."

"So, you are the movie star? Holy cats, this is my night! I'm a chauffeur for the stars!" hooted Crystal. "Now my mom is gonna freak! But listen Ma'am, I told him 'I didn't know any Lyla around Arcadia and I know everyone in town.' I don't think he believed me though, he kept snoopin' around and offerin' money to folks who could give him some info."

Crystal slowed to match the speed limit as she entered Zolfo Springs. An SUV was following closely behind. Smith had been watching in the rearview mirror but didn't say anything to the others.

In the Putt-Putt parking lot Ellwood was pulling on the door handles of the Porsche when someone behind him shouted, "Hey, I'm Jensen Hobson with Exclusive Entertainment Gossip News, E. E. G. I'm sure you've heard of us, we're the tell-all of the entertainment industry."

"Nope, never heard of ya," Ellwood answered as he broke into Lyla's Porsche with a tool he was trained to use at the Police Academy in Macon, Georgia.

"Well, anyway, I'm looking for Lyla Fontaine. Have you ever heard of her? We got a tip she was in this area yesterday and I'm thinking, since you're climbing into her car, that you may know something about her." The newsman paused and waited for a reply from Ellwood.

Ellwood climbed into the driver's seat and pushed it back as far as it would go to get his legs comfortably under the steering wheel. "Sorry, what were you sayin'?" he asked the reporter without making eye contact.

"I said" he began again, "I'm looking for Lyla Fontaine. We heard she was in this area yesterday and since you're in her car I think you may know something about her whereabouts?"

The glove compartment popped open when Ellwood hit the switch on the dash. He reached inside while Jensen continued his exasperating plea for more information on any Lyla Fontaine sightings in the area. He offered a tidy sum of money to Ellwood to spill the beans and was quite put out when the door was slammed shut, and Ellwood put his cell to his ear.

"Chief," he began in a far less monotone voice than he normally used, "I think there's a lot more going on here than just stolen golf carts."

"What now, Ellwood?"

"The Porsche was parked at the Putt-Putt. The movie star, the golfer, and the other gal are nowhere around, but I'm inside the Porsche..."

BANG! BANG!

"Hey knock it off!" Ellwood yelled.

"What's that? What's going on?" Chief Norton demanded.

"I've got some Hollywood reporter looking for Lyla Fontaine banging on the car window'" Ellwood explained to the Chief.

BANG! BANG! He pounded again and Chief Norton could hear his muffled voice demanding information about the star.

"Get out of here!" Ellwood yelled through the glass. He turned his attention back to the phone conversation while the reporter continued to pound the window, "There's a note in Lyla's Fontaine's glove box and it ain't fan mail."

"What does it say?" Chief Norton questioned over the cell phone.

Ellwood read out loud, "WE KNOW WHO YOU ARE LYLA FOUNTAINE HOW MUCH WILL YOU PAY TO KEEP IT SECRET WE'LL FIND YOU"

"Do you think Will and the chop shop boys are into more than swipin' golf carts?" Ellwood questioned. "Do you think they're trying to swindle this lady outa some cash?"

The Chief paused before answering, "I'm afraid it's time to call in the big guns, that sounds like a possible kidnapping threat. And guess what, if this is a kidnapping of an international star, it's above our pay grade. Robertson and Ramsey are on their way to Zolfo Springs in the unmarked car. They're gonna be calling for backup. Meet 'em there and bust Will, we've gotta get this wrapped up and find Lyla Fontaine before word gets out." Chief Norton ended his conversation on his cell and picked up the office phone to dial the FBI.

Jensen had stopped pounding on the Porsche in time to hear Ellwood read the note aloud to Chief Norton. He listened intently to what he could hear of their conversation and jotted some notes on a pad he pulled from his pocket.

The Porsche came to life causing the reporter to jump out of the way as Ellwood backed out to the road under the lime green sign glowing over Highway 70. He had found Lyla's spare key tucked away in the glove box with the ransom note and made a split-second decision to drive the sports car. It would get him to Zolfo Springs faster than any other vehicle, he rationalized as he sped toward the Arcadia city limits sign.

Jensen Hobson ran to his rented Tesla and followed the Porsche. His cell was dialing the personal cell phone of E.E.G.s senior editor. "Ralph," Jensen shouted into the phone set on speaker in the seat next to him, "Lyla Fontaine has been kidnapped and I'm in pursuit with the Arcadia police who are hunting down the kidnappers."

"Are you sure?" Ralph shouted back.

"Yup, I heard a guy reading the ransom note!" Jensen shouted back confidently.

"Stay on it, Jensen!" Ralph demanded. "We'll get the story started and do some digging from our end. Call me as soon as you know anything, good or bad."

The E.E.G. journalism staff tracked down a couple of phone numbers connected to Lyla Fontaine and began digging for more information. Betts was quietly studying her sermon for the upcoming Sunday when her cell rang with an unknown number. She considered answering but it was getting late so she let the call roll over to voicemail.

Chapter 26

Tracking the Club Car, the app on Smith's phone instructed Crystal to turn right at the next road. "No kidding," Smith whispered as she turned the Nissan under a wrought iron sign that read:

Vintage Lane Trailer and Mobile Home Park
No Speeding!

"I've driven past this place a hundred times or more and never had a very good feeling about it." Smith told the others in the car. He looked in the rearview mirror and could see the headlights of the SUV about a quarter of a mile behind them.

"Keep your eyes open and watch where we're going so we know how to get back out of here," Smith instructed, "I think we may be sandwiched in between the truck and trailer and someone in an SUV that has followed us since we left Arcadia."

"What are we going to do now that we're here?" Betty asked.

"Well, first I think we should text the pictures and video we took earlier tonight from our phones to someone else's phone, someone safe. All the evidence could be lost if the crooks commandeer our cells." Lyla suggested, remembering a scene from *James Bond in Shanghai*. In the movie, the only evidence against the evil Dr. Lourde was lost and James Bond had to retrieve it from behind enemy lines which took almost an hour and twenty minutes of the movie script. "We can text the evidence to someone who will keep it safe and if we need a bargaining chip in all of this, we've got it."

"Who should we text it to?" Betty asked.

"Text it to Betts," Lyla instructed.

Betts, home reclining in her La-Z-Boy, became curious as to why her phone continued to ding and buzz. The distraction prompted her to lay down her book and get a drink of cold ice water. On her way back to the La-Z-Boy she picked her cell up from the coffee table and checked the messages.

The first was a picture of a man she didn't recognize driving a golf cart past the Venus De Milo with a message from her mother in all caps: DO NOT DELETE!

The second was a video from Auntie Beatrice. She watched the same golf cart being loaded onto a trailer with a message that read: Keep safe for police!

Panic gripped Betts. She remembered the phone call that buzzed her phone around nine o'clock and checked for a voice message. "This is Ralph Burnett, editor and chief of E.E.G News. I hate to leave this message on voicemail but, we are trying to track down your mother, Lyla Fontaine, and have reason to believe she may be in some danger. We'd like to see her returned home safely. Could you give us a call back and we'll all cooperate with the authorities? My number is 555-600-NEWS."

Lyla's phone began vibrating in her purse. "Oh goodness, Betts is calling me," she sighed, "this is not a good time, dear," she said to the phone without answering. She turned it off and dropped it in her pocket.

Betty whispered, "You'd better call her later, she'll have a fit when she gets those pictures and figures out what we're doing!" Betty mocked a conversation, "Sorry Betts, can't talk, we're about to bust the thieves that swiped Smith's golf cart. We're going to make a citizen's arrest, so I'll get back to you in five or ten, okay? If you don't hear from us, though, could you give Officer Robby a message from me, 'told you so!'."

Crystal dimmed the headlights and inched over the bumpy slag past mobile homes with covered windows and doors tightly shut and locked. The only life evident in the park stirred within the first few trailers near the entrance, just inside the welcome sign. A porch light glowed from one and the light from a television flickered in another, but the deeper the Nissan traveled into the park, the darker it grew, except for the headlights of the SUV that had turned into the park and trailed a ways behind them. The Nissan rounded a bend and through the blackness Smith could make out a break in the wooden fence that lined the Vintage Lane Trailer Park property.

"Look," Smith whispered, "There's a building of some kind behind those shrubs. It looks like there might be lights on inside. Crystal, stop here. We'll get a couple more pictures."

"I'll get them and text them to Betts," Betty offered.

Crystal pushed the brake pedal to the floor and Betty, proudly clothed for the event, jumped out. Her spandex gave her full range of motion and she was able to crouch behind the bumper. She reached for Lyla's scarf to cover her head, but when it wasn't around her neck, she realized it was left behind in the Porsche. Thinking quickly on her tennis shoe clad feet, Betty opted to stoop behind a bush and aim her camera through the branches. The headlights of the SUV were slowly creeping down the road and in a matter of seconds the vehicle would round the bend and illuminate the sky-blue Nissan. She zoomed in on the target and snapped a burst of well-aimed shots but when she tried to jump back into the Nissan, her yoga pants were caught fast to an overgrown Bougainvillea.

"I'm caught! My yoga pants are caught in a thorn bush," Betty panicked.

"Strip them off and get in the car, Betty, there are headlights coming around the bend." Lyla shouted.

"I WILL NOT, Lyla! I would rather be taken hostage than carry out a sting half dressed! Especially with Smith in the car." Betty tugged on her pant leg but couldn't rip it free. "I bought the pants with the tightest weave, dog-gone-it, I didn't want unsightly cellulite distracting me. I didn't know they would be the death of me!"

Lyla scolded her, "Yoga pants are always a bad choice, dear!"

"Crystal, get out of here," Betty commanded, "I'll hide in the Bougainvillea and get my pant leg free while you circle around. When the SUV is gone, come pick me up!"

"I can't leave..." Crystal began but Betty cut her off,

"GO! GO! GO!"

Crystal obeyed and pulled forward easing the Nissan slowly around a bend in the gravel road leaving Betty held captive by the Bougainvillea. She brought the car to a stop behind a darkened trailer and Smith reached across the dash, flipped off the lights and whispered to turn off the engine. The SUV had turned into the

Vintage Trailer Park and was quietly inching along the gravel following the fence line as the Nissan had done only moments earlier. Lyla gasped when its headlights stopped in front of the bougainvillea bush. Quiet voices could be heard but were inaudible, drowned out by the hissing and rattling of machinery in the building behind the fence.

"What are they saying? Can you make out their words?" Lyla pleaded as Crystal and Smith both opened their doors and leaned into the night. As they strained to make out the conversation another car turned in under the hanging "Welcome" sign causing it to creak.

"My goodness, this is a busy place," Smith whispered.

The second car entered and the three watched as the lowriding headlights went dark after crawling only a short distance down the gravel road. It pulled in behind a doublewide and stopped. The only sounds in the night came from the building behind the fence.

"I've got a plan," Lyla started, "I was in a situation like this in the movie James Bond Iced in Alaska. Bond was trapped and I had to rescue him."

"I remember that movie," Smith exclaimed, "You caught the illegal whalers by surprise. They had no idea you were on the ship, so you used the element of surprise as a distraction. It was masterful!"

Lyla was thrilled he had remembered her scene, "Why thank you, Smith" She smiled in the dark before she continued, "Yes, I did, and I threw them off just long enough for James Bond to make a break for it. I think we can rush in and startle those thugs and scare them off. That'll give Betty and her yoga pants a few seconds to get out of there."

The three quickly strategized and deployed to their positions keeping a darkened trailer between them and the SUV. While Lyla took a moment to recall some of her lines from that scene before they made their move, a third car turned into the trailer parked and stopped directly under the "Welcome" sign.

"We'd better bust Ms. Brown oughta here before the place gets too crowded," Crystal whispered. "Do your Hollywood thing, Ms. Anne or Ms. Lyla, whoever you are."

Lyla paused and remembered her character's lines, "Halt!" she yelled as deep and as threatening as she was able.

"Quiet out here," a voice hissed.

"I want to hear my friend's voice or we're coming in after her." Lyla shouted back.

"Lyla," Betty called, "it's me. Be quiet!"

"You can't make me be quiet, I'm locked and loaded and ready for bear. We're coming in!" Lyla hoped these Floridians understood as well as the Alaskans in the movie that with that line, she meant business. She winced a bit thinking the hoodlums may have been more frightened if she would have shouted that she was locked and loaded for gators rather than bear.

"Lyla, hush," came Betty's voice through the darkness, "I'm with Robby!"

"WHAT?" Smith stepped out from behind the trailer.

"Get back, all of you," Officer Robertson commanded.

The door to the building swung wide and the light from within poured into the dark trailer park. David Willoughby's silhouette swayed side-to-side as he moved from the building closer to the gravel road.

Officer Robertson shouted to the group a second time, "Get out of here!"

But Lyla, Smith, and Crystal all stood frozen beside the trailer confused by what was happening.

David Willoughby fired a shot from a rifle into the air, "Who's out there?" he yelled without a trace of a British accent.

Officer Robertson barked back, "Give it up Will. We got ya, no need to try to fight, back-up is coming. McCoy is on his way."

And at that moment, just as Robby Robertson finished his sentence and drew a breath, four armored SWAT team vehicles barreled into The Vintage Lane Trailer Park. A loud crunching was heard as the first black Hummer pushed a Tesla out of their way. Two of the vehicles spun gravel as they veered to the left of the circle and two to the right thundering past the silver Porsche that was tucked safely behind a double-wide off the road. One truck sideswiped a steel post at the entrance and set the wrought iron "Welcome" sign swinging so hard the "e" side of the sign broke free from the rust laden hook that had held it hanging at a slight tilt. Screeching to a stop the four vehicles emptied. Twenty-one, heavily armed SWAT team officers in full riot gear, exploded from the trucks and surrounded the area. The four team drivers remained inside the cockpits and manned the flood lights that blinded David Willoughby and brought him to his knees.

Lyla screamed for Betty. Smith dropped and covered his head with his hands. And Crystal Bell could be heard shouting, "Go get 'em boys!"

"Come out with your hands up, we've got you surrounded!" blasted from the loudspeaker in the lead truck as a helicopter appeared and circled above blazing a spotlight that illuminated the entire scene unfolding at the Vintage Trailer Park.

SWAT stormed the old structure behind the hedges. Fourteen men, including undercover agent Benny Alberts and one woman were pulled from the chop shop.

"There's Susan!" Smith pointed. "I would have never thought it..."

Benny was released by the information SWAT received from Chief Norton. He found Officer Robertson immediately, "Hey, Robby," he said dusting himself off, "SWAT for Will and his boys is a bit of overkill, isn't it?"

The SWAT team captain ordered David Willoughby to drop face down and while he yanked the handcuffs into place he yelled, "Where's Lyla Fontaine, Willoughby?" Pulling him to his feet the captain repeated the question, "I said, where's the actress, Willoughby?"

"I got no idea what you're talkin' about," Willoughby growled spitting dirt from between his teeth.

Robby flashed his badge to the SWAT team, "She's somewhere here in the trailer park, she's safe with the golfer, Smith Kennedy and a teenager named Crystal Bell. I know it sounds crazy but welcome to Arcadia! I've got her friend in the SUV over there to explain the whole story."

Ellwood McCoy called out to Lyla as he approached the group from behind, "Ms. Fontaine, are you alright? We had a report you were kidnapped. It looks like they sent the pros to rescue you."

Smith, Lyla and Crystal turned. "Ellwood? Ellwood McCoy?" Smith stammered.

"In the flesh, sort of. My real name is Brad Keys, I'm an undercover officer. They put me in the Village to be the inside man in the golf cart ring then you two moved in and doubled my assignment, especially when you started putting two-and-two together about the stolen carts. You're a couple of sharp old cookies." he chuckled. "Are the three of you ok?" he asked again.

"So, you knew who we were all along?" Smith asked.

Officer Brad Keys explained, "Well, pretty much, Herb Lewis tipped us off when you both moved into the Village the same week. He asked for extra security to keep the press away. We did some investigating, but we wanted to keep things low-key until the golf cart theft ring was broken. We couldn't take the chance of a lot of press showing up and scaring Willoughby off before we got him. The two of you and Ms. Brown kept me on my toes!"

Bond-girl, Lyla Fontaine became weak in the knees and began to grow faint. Brad grabbed her arm and supported her under the elbow. "We're over here," he hollered across the park to Robby. "Ms. Fontaine may need a little help right now."

Smith steadied Lyla by leaning her against him as he held her other arm and Crystal ran to Betty.

The SWAT team captain called for a stretcher for Lyla. She sat down on the portable bed to regain her bearings, "Really, thank you all, but I'm alright. I was just unsteady for a moment in all of the commotion." A blood pressure cuff was pushed up on her arm.

Betty shoved through the crowd. Wrapping her arms around her friend she teased, "Lyla Fontaine, this is not the way someone with a heart condition should spend their evening."

"Oh Betty, I was so worried about you, you brave thing." Lyla embraced Betty and breathed a deep sigh of relief. "I would never have been able to live with myself if I had let anything happen to you while you were squeezed into that pair of yoga pants!" Then turning to Officer Robertson, she added, "I'm so thankful you were here, Robby. So thankful you rescued my friend from the thorn bushes and all things terrible in this place tonight!"

"Your pressure is a little high but completely normal for what you've been through, Ma'am. I'm sure the whole event just shook you up," the SWAT team medic assured Lyla. "You go on home and get some sleep. We'll tell the Arcadia police to take your statements in the morning and let you rest. They're going to be busy with Willoughby tonight anyway."

Smith grabbed Betty's shoulders but then let his arms wrap around her in a bear hug, "That was the bravest thing I have ever seen anyone do, including James Bond. You are my hero Betty Brown." He kissed her cheek before he released her.

A member of the SWAT team burst through the ring of protection around Lyla, "I found this fellow sneaking around with a camera, taking pictures." He held the reporter by the collar.

"Hey!" Crystal shouted at the young man, "How'd you get here?"

"You're lucky you didn't get yourself killed, fella," Officer Keys shook his head at the man disgusted at the lengths the guy would go to get a story.

"Jensen? I can't believe it! Have you tracked Lyla all the way to Arcadia?" Betty was shocked to see the man in the custody of the SWAT team. "Lyla, you remember Jensen Hobson. I should have figured you'd be the reporter on the story when we heard that E.E.G. was snooping around." She raised an eyebrow and cocked her head to one side, "So, did you get the shots you wanted?"

"Oh man, I'm asking for a bonus for what I have here," Jensen confessed. "I got the whole show right here," he held up his camera and waved in the air. "The movie star, the golfer, the SWAT team, the local police, and the crooks! Baby, this is worth a fortune."

Lyla stopped him, "Hold on, Jensen."

"Ms. Fontaine, this will finance my retirement, don't go trying to make deals."

Lyla began again, "Jensen, before you send any pictures, I promise you, I'll make it worth your while if you do just two little things for me."

"And if you help me with a little something, I'll jump in on this deal with Lyla," Smith added.

"Well, I guess it will depend on what these two-plus-one-more little things are," Jensen answered as he was released from the grip of the rather large SWAT team officer.

"It appears that you don't have a car to get out of here tonight, dear," Lyla smiled looking back at the Tesla wrinkled up against a trailer, "I'm going to have Officer Brad drive my Porsche back to the police station, since he helped himself to it earlier and drove it out here, so the only ride back to Arcadia tonight would be with us in the Nissan. We can talk on the way."

Robby encouraged him, "That's probably going to be your best offer, buddy."

Officer Robertson asked Lyla, Smith, Betty, and Crystal to meet at the Arcadia Police Department at 10:00 a.m. the next morning to take their statements.

"I think I'd better call my mom and dad, it's gettin' kinda late." Crystal was looking at the time on her phone as the group of victorious detectives prepared to leave the scene of the crime. "I'm gonna let them know I'm on my way home but first I have to drop off Lyla Fontaine, Smith Kennedy and a bona fide Hollywood reporter."

"Do you think they'll believe you?" Smith asked.

"If they don't, I'll just tell 'em to turn on the eleven o'clock news!" she giggled.

Lyla Fontaine and Smith Kennedy both shook hands and took selfies with the SWAT team before they drove the armored vehicles back out to the highway. Betty got into the Nissan and sat up front with Crystal while Lyla and Smith climbed in with Jensen Hobson in the middle of the back seat between them.

Betts's car was parked in Lyla's driveway when Crystal pulled up to the cottage. Smith suggested that they all get out and take a picture with Crystal as proof to her parents she really did spend an evening rescuing a movie star and professional golfer. Smith called as she backed out onto Sunset Lane, "Call me if you need my help with an explanation, it's the least I can do since we haven't found you a cowboy, yet."

"Thanks, boss," Crystal snickered, "see you in the A.M."

A few of the Villagers who lingered at the arena until the last event was scored were just arriving home from the rodeo. It was a disappointing first evening. Jake The Jerk was trailing in points behind a cowboy no one had even heard of before this year's competition.

"We hope you all had a better evening then we did," Sam hollered out to the group in Lyla's drive, "What a letdown."

Betts came running from the cottage when she heard voices. "Mother! Are you ok?" I came as soon as I got the call from E.E.G. Why didn't you call me, or answer your phone when I called you? I was frantic."

"Oh, Betts, why did E.E.G. call you?" Lyla asked.

"To tell me you were in danger and possibly kidnapped! I thought you had been kidnapped by a group of ruffians who were going to...to harm you." Betts teared up at the mention of her mother in danger.

"I don't know why everyone thought I was kidnapped but it was very kind of them to send a SWAT team to my rescue," Lyla said with a yawn.

"I called the police and they had a threatening note that was found in the glove box of the Porsche. Oh, Momma, I was so frightened for you. Officer Norton told me to come to the police station during the rescue. I sat with him until we got the word that you were found." Betts hugged her mother. "I would have just died if you had been hurt. That Crystal, I'm going to have a word with her, she was to keep you out of danger, not drive you headlong into it!"

Lyla dragged her weary body up the three front steps into the house and didn't stop until she was laying on her bed.

Chapter 27

Lyla and Betts left the house at 9:30 a.m. to pick up Smith and Betty on their way to the Arcadia Police Department. They all knew 3.2 miles would be almost impossible to make in thirty minutes. The press was held at bay outside of the Arcadia Retirement Village gate but the golf cart path along the stucco wall was packed with cameras and news reporters spilling into the road. Every network on the continent and few from overseas had someone on site begging for a statement from Lyla Fontaine and Smith Kennedy.

"Tell us about the kidnapping, Lyla."

"Are you going back to Hollywood, Ms. Fontaine?"

"Smith, is that your Putt-Putt?"

"Did the two of you plan to meet here?"

"Lyla, what are you doing in Arcadia?"

Microphones were waved at the windows of Betts's car and camera operators ran down the road next to them. Lyla waved and smiled, and Smith tipped his golf hat but neither responded keeping their promise to Jensen Hobson.

Johnson called his dad on his way into town, "Well old man, looks like you've done it again. The streets are so packed I can hardly get through. If I can get there, I'll just meet you at the police station."

Smith had called Johnson as he dropped into bed at midnight. He wanted his son to have a rundown of the events of the past few weeks before the press got wind of the story and it became headline news in the morning. He began the tale with setting up the sting by playing the part of Betty Brown's boyfriend then he finished with a restrained report of the SWAT team rescue. Johnson could hear the exhaustion in his dad's voice. "I'm glad you're okay, old man. Get some sleep and I'll run up to Arcadia first thing in the morning and go to the police station with you. I'm not going to sleep a wink tonight after that story. Man, I can't wait to hear the details."

Stuck in the traffic jamming Highway 70, Lyla's cell buzzed, her caller ID displayed Crystal's number. "Hello, dear," she answered putting Crystal on speaker.

"Ms. Lyla, can you help me, please?" she begged.

"Of course, Crystal, what's wrong?" Lyla answered.

"I have no idea what to tell all the reporters outside my house standin' in my driveway." Crystal giggled, "This is just the craziest thing that ever happened to me. I have no idea what to tell 'em or how to act so my momma and daddy said to call you and ask the professional."

"Well Crystal, put on your best outfit and do your hair, you are about to be seen on millions of TV's around the world!"

Crystal hooted over the speaker phone.

"Then take your daddy by the arm and step out there with your sweetest smile. Now here's the most important tip, my professional advice to you, are you ready?" Lyla asked.

"Yes Ma'am, I sure am," Crystal poised herself for the advice.

"Ignore EVERYTHING they say and ask. Just wave your hand and tell them all, 'No comment'. Remember, we have a promise to keep." Lyla hung up and smiled.

Police officers from cities all throughout DeSoto County were called to help with traffic flow and crowd control. Betts's car was stopped by an officer holding her hands out in front of her, palms facing Betts as she crept along Highway 70. Coming to a full stop, the officer approached the car, "Ma'am, can you use another route? We have celebrities in town here and we need to clear the area to get them through."

Lyla and Smith leaned up from the backseat and merely smiled. "Oh, man, sorry Mr. Kennedy, Ms.

Fontaine." the officer apologized, "Wait right here, will you?"

"I hate to block traffic," Betts started but the officer was already speaking into the microphone on her lapel.

Within seconds, an officer on horseback arrived, swung his leg over the saddle and hopped to the ground. Betts lowered the window again as he came to the car. He tipped his hat and leaned in the window, "Ma'am, Sir, it would be an honor to be your escort to the station."

"Thank you, Officer Heinze," Smith said reading the young man's badge.

"Sir," Lyla interjected, "What's your horse's name?"

"Leroy" Officer Heinze answered with a smile and with that, he returned to the saddle and waved for them to follow.

Before Betts rolled the driver's window up Lyla called for the woman officer to come back to the window, "There will be another celebrity arriving in a sky-blue Nissan. I'm not sure if you've heard of her, but her name is Crystal Bell. She will need an escort to the Arcadia Police Department as well. Thank you, dear."

"Got it Ma'am, will do," the officer replied.

"Brilliant! Absolutely brilliant, Lyla!" Betty laughed at the thought of Crystal's reaction to a police escort through crowds of fans and reporters. "The girl will never be the same!"

Betts followed Officer Heinze atop Leroy to the Police Department. Reporters rushed the car as it pulled into the parking lot and Leroy was maneuvered between the crowd and the car making room for the four passengers to get to the building. Lyla and Smith stopped shy of the door and turned and waved.

"Ms. Fontaine, were you kidnapped?"

"Hey Kennedy, aren't you a little old for rescuing damsels in distress?"

Both returned the same reply, "No comment."

Officer Robertson met them at the door, "This is exactly what we didn't want to happen before Will and his boys were caught."

Smith interrupted before Robby could continue, "But, all's well that ends well, Robby!"

Jensen Hobson had spent the night at a B&B only two blocks from the Putt-Putt and walked to the Police Station earlier to hand over the incriminating photos to the Arcadia police. He met Lyla and Smith in the lobby, "We're good?"

"You bet," Smith answered, "as long as you hold up your end of the deal."

"I'm good with that," Jensen agreed. "I okayed everything with Ralph Clute, my senior editor, last night. But I need to complete the deal ASAP."

Crystal came bursting through the station door with her father and mother close behind. "Did you see that?

They gave me a police escort! And the people out there are asking me how I know you two and they're crazy! They're all crazy!" She shouted, "I love this!"

Her dad put his hand on her shoulder to quiet her. Introductions were made all around before Chief Norton asked the group to meet in the conference room. Family members were instructed to help themselves to coffee and donuts and wait in the lobby.

"Robby, my son is coming. His name is Johnson Kennedy..."

"You named a kid Johnson Kennedy, that's like, child abuse sir. You should have been arrested for that," Robby joked.

"Yup! That is exactly what my son thinks, too," Smith laughed with the officer. "He's coming, can you make sure he gets in?"

Chief Norton instructed everyone to sit around a large wooden conference table in the middle of the room and explained that everything said would be recorded on camera as he pointed to a lens mounted on the wall. He also noted that the evidence against David Willoughby would be held for the trial and anyone in the room could be subpoenaed but that would be unlikely. However, their meeting, at that time, would be to iron out the facts and the timeline. If anyone had any questions, now would be the time to ask. Chief Norton also warned that while the investigation and trial were in process anyone discussing evidence or facts outside the courtroom could be brought up on charges.

Jensen's photography was spectacular. He had photos of the SWAT team infiltrating the trailer park with the helicopter circling overhead. Lyla, Smith, and Crystal were photographed hiding in the shadows of the trailer and then coming into full view under the SWAT team flood lights.

Crystal requested a few prints be made of her with Lyla and Smith. Lyla noted her favorite shot was of David Willoughby in handcuffs.

"Willoughby has been on the run for years," Chief Norton explained. "He started with stolen cars, but they became too easy to trace, so a few years he back started a golf cart theft ring in Arizona under the name Tony LeNore."

"He's not from London, is he?" Betty asked.

"Nope." The Chief continued, "He and his boys created a chop shop and sold parts and refurbished carts for cash and made a killing out west. When the police there started to put the squeeze on the gang, he moved the operation to Florida and took the alias David Willoughby. He worked a lot of areas before he showed up in Arcadia. Officer Robertson tracked the missing carts and headed a sting to set him up. Herb Lewis worked with us and introduced Robby to the residents as a part-time guy. For the most part it worked great until a couple of celebrities showed up and started to put two-and-two together causing a whole lot of trouble!"

"Well, he certainly had us all fooled, I hate to admit it but I kind of liked the guy," Smith confessed.

"Who was the frightening man wearing plaid and blue jeans driving the old pick-up?" Lyla asked.

"Benny? He's special forces. He came to us from Mississippi. We had to have someone from out of town come in looking for quick money. Benny barreled into town in that beat-up old truck and four days into it was spotted by a couple of antique shoppers."

Lyla and Betty chuckled remembering the chase. Betty spoke out loud, "If Lyla didn't have James Bond in her blood, she never would have chased him! We would have acted like a couple of old women, fainted on the spot, and forgotten the whole thing because of 'some-timers'. But Lyla was and always will be a Bond girl, you know."

"Ms. Fontaine, Ms. Brown, I need to ask your forgiveness for roughing you up the day you came in to meet with Robby," Chief Norton said apologetically.

Lyla wrinkled her brow and pursed her lips, "Oh my dear, I was not happy with you that day, but I totally understand, now. You are forgiven, Chief." Lyla's eyes traveled from person to person around the room, "You should all be in the movies, every one of you. What superb actors!"

Chief Norton took on a serious tone, "Ms. Fontaine, you need to know that we were worried for your life. You never know what someone like Willoughby is capable of. When Keys found the note in the glove box of your Porsche, we didn't know where that came from or what might happen to you. Who threatened you like that?"

"Fans get a bit ridiculous and demanding. I insisted to a couple of fellows that I was Anne Knight and I'm sure they left that note on my windshield." Lyla raised her hands, palm lifted up in an expression of indifference, "I've lived with those idle threats most of my career."

Smith turned everyone's attention to Jensen. "Our E.E.G. reporter has cut a deal with us and we want to inform all of you about the details. Lyla and I have agreed to allow Jensen full release of any photos to the press that the police deem acceptable. We have agreed to grant him an exclusive story, our full story, to be printed by E.E.G. and its subsidiaries in up-coming editions. We will also prepare an exclusive television interview with him; however, he must uphold his part of the agreement, correct Jensen?"

Jensen agreed publicly in front of the witnesses in the room, "That is correct."

Chief Norton asked, "What have you agreed to?"

Jensen began, "I had offered to buy information concerning the whereabouts of Lyla Fontaine. It has been agreed upon that the money E.E.G. had made available for this project be placed in a trust fund for Miss Crystal Bell. It will be accessible only for college tuition and accessed by the university of her choice."

Robby was curious, "What were you prepared to offer?"

Jensen answered, "Fifty grand." Crystal let out a whoop that everyone in the lobby could hear.

Jensen turned to Betty, "We also agree to keep the name 'Beatrice Brown' out of the media. We understand that Ms. Brown is a private citizen and we wish to protect her from the onslaught of the chaos we are witnessing in Arcadia today."

Betty breathed a deep sigh of relief, "Jensen, you are a dear. Thank Ralph for me, will you?"

"Of course, Beatrice," Jensen smiled kindly, feeling good about himself for putting her above the story. He tried to remember if he had ever done that before and decided this was a first for him.

"That was two, what's the third thing?" Chief Norton asked.

"Smith will have me help him with a project," Jensen answered.

"For years I drove past the Vintage Trailer Park in Zolfo Springs and always thought I should do something to spruce the place up a bit and make it homier and more welcoming, but I never did."

"Well, I'm not sure you're going to be able to spruce it up much, there's not a lot left of it now," Robby commented.

"Right, so I should be able to buy it at a fair price and rebuild," Smith explained, "And Jensen is going to help with the brochure and the marketing."

"Oh, Smith," Lyla giggled, "You're going to redecorate the trailer park, just like the Putt-Putt." She smiled revealing the small space between her teeth then winked.

Chapter 28

"Let's get going,' Smith yelled to Johnson, "We need to get there to get a parking spot and a place to sit."

"We're going to be an hour early, Dad, slow down man," Johnson gurgled while spitting his toothpaste into the sink under the running water.

The entire detective entourage planned to sit front row in the Wesley United Methodist Church of New Smyrna Beach and worship together Easter morning. The Reverend Betts Knight had announced to her congregation that Lyla Fontaine and Smith Kennedy, along with the accomplices that helped bust the golf cart theft ring everyone was talking about, would all be worshiping in the front row on Easter Sunday and be available for autographs in the parking lot after the service. She prayed for forgiveness for manipulating her flock by using the two stars as a motivation to fill the church with family and friends, but she knew without a doubt this would be the biggest Easter turnout in church history.

When Lyla arrived with Betty the parking lot was already overflowing into a neighboring plaza. Rev. Betts had thought ahead and had her assistant Ruth block off four parking spaces outside and reserve the front pew inside for the guests. Lyla parked the silver Porsche in the reserved spot closest to the big wooden doors opened to the church sanctuary. She and Betty looked exquisite in their Easter attire as the light morning breeze caught the hem of their dresses waving them slightly. Knowing pictures would be taken with paparazzi present, both donned spring colors recommended by Lyla's fashion advisor and designed by Louis Vuitton.

When Crystal and her parents arrived, she immediately spied the silver Porsche. "Park there, Dad, next to Ms. Lyla and the boss can park on the other side of us." Her parents mused at their daughter's familiarity with the world-renowned celebrities. Inside the sanctuary Crystal hugged the two women, "Golly, Arcadia just idn't gonna be the same without the two of you paired up and bustin' villains," she giggled. "I'm gonna miss you, Ms. Lyla. I hope you'll be planning a visit back to us."

Johnson pulled on his suit jacket and loosened the top button on his shirt, glad he hadn't worn a tie. He climbed out of the Highlander feeling pleased to be headed back into a church keeping the promise he had made when his dad was in the ICU. This was just

the beginning, he reminded himself
church in Naples as soon as he could

Smith pulled himself from the p
took a long look at the stately wh
beautiful day to celebrate new beginnings, he thought.
Resurrection Sunday, the day of new life. He breathed a thank you to God and sucked in the fresh morning air. New life filled his soul and an excitement for all that was to come brought a smile to his face.

Before the two men could step into the sanctuary, a van marked Arcadia Police Department on the door pulled into the last slot available next to the Highlander. Officer Robby, Chief Norton, and officers Benny and Brad piled out. "Hey, Kennedy, wait up," Robby shouted. They jogged to catch up and shook hands with the father and son pair.

The group of celebrities were an impressive sight sitting shoulder to shoulder in the pew, but it was the church altar that took the worshipers' breath away. White Easter lilies stood tall in full bloom around a rugged, wooden cross draped in white, a magnificent reminder of the death and resurrection of the Savior of the world, Jesus.

Reverend Betts requested all available ushers bring extra chairs from the fellowship hall and set them in the back of the church and in the aisles, leaving just enough space for congregants to pass by. When the room began rflowing, chairs were set in the entry, the hallway and finally in the parking lot.

At ten o'clock sharp, the worship leader stood and shouted, "God is good!"

The congregation returned with, "All the time!"

He raised his voice again, "And all the time!"

And the congregation shouted back, "GOD IS GOOD!"

"Then let's praise this good God of ours!" He called out and the worship team broke into song. It was an Easter service like none other. Praise could be heard ringing into the parking lot and down the street. Passengers in cars stopped at the traffic light in the road rolled down their windows and listened to the joy bubbling out the opened doors of the grand white church with the overflowing parking lot.

Reverend Betts, led by the Spirit, preached the resurrection message of redemption to the glory of God. At the conclusion, she prayed for the salvation of those who didn't know Jesus as their Savior, yet. With eyes closed throughout the congregation, she echoed the words she had prayed with Pastor James at the Baptist Episcopal Methodist Church years back.

There wasn't room to open the altar area, so she invited everyone to just accept Jesus right there in their seats as the worship leader played, *I Surrender All* quietly on the keyboard.

Quiet sniffling was heard as she concluded the prayer with a joyful "Amen."

The service closed and everyone stood singing, "He lives, He lives, He lives within my heart!"

An umbrella was set up outside the big wooden doors and the entourage of crime fighters greeted the congregants, signed autographs and snapped a multitude of selfies. The police officers lingered and shook a few hands but stood back from the limelight of the attention. Crystal Bell, on the other hand, embraced the moment and devoured the attention. She hooted out loud every time she was asked to sign an autograph book.

Of course, most everyone wanted to greet Lyla and Smith and a large crowd formed around the two. A small elderly lady waited quietly in line to meet her favorite Bond girl, Lyla Fontaine. The woman's wrinkled hand trembled as she held out her bulletin and asked, "Will you sign this, please?"

"Of course," Lyla responded cheerfully. "I'm so glad you're here today."

The lady smiled back, "I'm glad you're here. A friend told me you would be here today, so I came to meet you in person, and I met Jesus in person, too."

Lyla hugged the woman. "I don't believe I've ever been a part of introducing someone to Jesus, before." She pulled her own bulletin from her purse, "Could I have your autograph?" The lady's signature was faint and shaky, but Lyla could make out the name Anne Thompson, "Thank you Anne, I shall always remember your name. Anne, it's a name that will always signify a new beginning for me."

The crowd retreated to their cars one after another and hurried home to enjoy their Easter dinners and egg hunts. Officer Robertson stepped under the umbrella with Smith and Lyla. He shook the hand of Smith Kennedy and appreciated the God given talent that graced those very hands. "It was good to meet you, sir. I'll keep an eye on Claire's Putt-Putt and look for you when you're in town."

Smith smiled, "Hey, Robby. I'm sorry that I fibbed and didn't tell you who I really was right from the start."

Robby chuckled, "No worries, all's well that ends well, you know!"

Officer Robert Robertson approached Lyla, removed his police hat with one hand and took hers in the other. Lyla felt the burning of tears welling up in her eyes. "Oh Robby, I still thank the good Lord that you were right there with us that night. He sent you as an angel to watch over a couple of crazy old Bond girls, you know. God bless you."

The police officer wiped his eye and wrapped his arm around the shoulder of the great Lyla Fontaine. "Take care of yourself out in Hollywood. I won't be there to keep my eye on you!" His throat began to tighten, "I'm gonna miss you, Ma'am." The officers shook hands all around and disappeared into the Arcadia Police Department van.

In grand Lyla Fontaine fashion, Lyla stood on the steps of the church and waved her wrap to draw everyone's attention and announced she would be hosting a dinner party to honor her friends and partners in crime busting. "Every one of you are invited," she paused and pulled her blue sunglasses over the edge of her nose and declared, "and you all are expected."

Crystal sighed, "Sounds nice, Ms. Lyla, but I won't ever be able to get to Hollywood, Ma'am."

Lyla looked shocked at the girl's reaction, "Don't think you're getting out of one of my dinner parties that easily, young lady. I'll send a jet for you!"

Crystal clapped her hands and hugged Lyla, "I haven't ever had friends like y'all!! Y'all make it seem like the older ya get, the better ya get!"

Betts checked to be sure the church doors were shut and locked. "Let's get you back to my house Momma and ready to fly home to Beverly Hills tomorrow."

As they walked to the parking lot Lyla, Smith and Betty trailed behind Johnson and Betts who were laughing as they exchanged childhood stories about being raised by famous parents.

The trio stopped at the Porsche and hugged, recounting the highlights of their wild adventure.

"I'll see you both again soon," Lyla kissed Smith on the cheek first then Betty. Smith opened the door of the Porsche for her and she slid into the driver's seat, pulled her blue rimmed sunglasses from the top of her head and let her silver curls bounce around her shoulders.

He moved to the back of the car where Betty stood waiting to say their good-byes, "I've been thinking," Smith said as he reached out and put his hand on Betty's shoulder.

Betty raised an eyebrow, "Smith Kennedy, that can be quite dangerous."

"Well," he continued, "You're probably right, this could get dangerous. I kind of enjoyed pretending to be your boyfriend and I thought we might try the real thing?" He paused, "I'll be in Arcadia quite a bit getting Claire's Putt-Putt Golf set to run without me there every day and well, I'd like to take you to dinner."

Lyla leaned her head out the window, "Just say 'yes,' Beatrice. Accept the man's offer!"

"Hmmm," Betty tilted her head and squinted at him as if to consider his intentions, "You've got my number, why don't you call me and I'll plan it out in bullet points," she teased and slid into the passenger seat.

The silver Porsche backed out of the parking space and turned toward the highway with Lyla driving and blazing like a supernova.

THE END

Epilogue

I hope you have found yourself somewhere in this story. Are you the risk-taking Lyla Fontaine or are you Smith Kennedy battling to get back the life you're afraid of losing? Maybe you are Betty Brown, content to live out your days in a quiet and peaceful retirement.

Whomever you might identify with in *Lyla's Encore,* the character was someone who was willing to allow the needs of others to interrupt his or her life.

Who needs you today?

Is there someone in your life that needs you (not a SWAT team) to swoop in and save them with a word of encouragement and hope? Is there a grandchild longing for a listening ear or a coworker searching for a thoughtful friend? It's very possible that a small plate of cookies could be the prescription that heals the heart of a grieving neighbor.

Look for the myriad of God-given opportunities to make a difference in the lives of the people in your sphere of influence. Anticipate these types of interruptions, daily. And as you do, be ready to see the results, because you, dear friends will change your world, however big or small your world may be.

CPSIA information can be obtained
at www.ICGtesting.com
Printed in the USA
LVHW050607141020
668672LV00002B/165